Trouble in Tawas

Madison Johns

Copyright © 2013 by Madison Johns

Trouble in Tawas Madison John

This e-book is licensed for your personal enjoyment only. This e-book may not be re-sold or given away to other people. If you would like to share this book with another person, please purchase an additional copy for each recipient. If you're reading this book and did not purchase it, or it was not purchased for your use only, then please purchase your own copy. Thank you for respecting the hard work of this author

Disclaimer: This is a work of fiction. Any similarity to persons living or dead (unless explicitly noted) is merely coincidental.

Edited by http://ebookeditingpro.com/
Proofreader Jason Sinner
Book cover by http://www.coverkicks.com/
Beta reader Mary Sorenson

Acknowledgment

I'd like to thank all of my readers and fans of my Agnes Barton mystery series and also for my Facebook friends who have supported me.

Special thanks to Susan Coils who made some of the most awesome covers ever.
You have captured Agnes and Eleanor perfectly and I can't thank you enough!

Dedication

I dedicate this book to my children Andrea and Luke who have lost so much, but still are my shining stars.

Other books by Madison Johns

Coffin Tales Season of Death
Armed and Outrageous
Grannies, Guns and Ghosts
Senior Snoops
Treasure in Tawas
Pretty, Hip & Dead
Pretty and Preagnant
Redneck Romance

Chapter One

I carried my mail from the post office to the campground where I had been living for the last year in East Tawas, Michigan—in a Winnebago no less. It was quite the walk, but at seventy-two a body needs to do as much exercising as possible.

I had just returned from Florida for the winter; a trip that Sheriff Peterson had set up. Just our luck, my fellow sleuthing buddy Eleanor and I solved a case while down there.

I'm Agnes Barton and I'm what folks in town call a senior sleuth. My house has just been rebuilt after it was firebombed, and I'm waiting on the inspectors—something to do with a snag with the building permit. All I know is, they are moving slower than molasses and they are testing my patience. My sidekick, Eleanor Mason, is eighty-two and quite a handful. She lives in a beach house directly on Lake Huron.

East Tawas is situated on Lake Huron, with a nice sized dock where yachts moored from spring to late fall. The campground is directly behind the bait shop, and that is where I've been staying. No tents are allowed. It's all campers, including a black one owned by the gypsy, Leotyne Williams—someone who saved my life via a magical necklace, or so I thought. We're still trying to get used to each other, and I hate to admit it, but she freaks me out! She even has one of those hell hounds that happens to be afraid of cats.

I made way into my camper, and my cat, Duchess, was howling something fierce. "What is *your* problem now, Duchess?"

I spied her empty dish and proceeded to fill it with a can of tuna. I wished I had never started that habit. She now thinks she deserves a can every morning for breakfast.

The interior of my camper was purple and pink. That's what I get for buying it at a police auction. My counter tops were beige granite with flecks of black. I had painted the cupboards eggshell white to tone down the brightness of the purple walls and pink couches and dinette seats. I replaced the purple table with an oak one. It still shone from the lacquer finish.

I passed a mirror and smoothed my salt and pepper hair into place. I was one lucky duck for having a thick head of hair, but creases lined my face that most people would consider wrinkles. Most of them were around my mouth, but I still sported full, cherry red lips. I had slipped on blue crop pants and white sandals, with a matching white tee with a tiny emblem of an anchor, hastily this morning in hopes of getting an early start.

I sat the mail down, then shuffled through it until I came across a flyer. My eyes widened when I saw that it was a political flyer for Sheriff Clem Peterson. I had said for years that I would cause a stir at his re-election bid, and now was my chance. I slumped down in my seat. "Duchess, what should I do?" She looked up at me and blinked, as if to signal me to call my best friend Eleanor Mason, but I had already planned to visit her that day. Now was as good a time as any, so I ambled out the door, taking care as I descended the steps. The last thing I needed in my life was to fall and break a hip. Lord knows my hip had been acting up for years, but thus far, I had been spared the knife.

I got into my red Mustang, and once the engine roared to life, I tooled out of the campground and on to US 23. Bathing suit clad beach-goers whizzed past on motorcycles, and I smiled. Sheriff Peterson hated motorcycles in town—too many flashbacks from the seventies, perhaps. As for me, I knew they were kids, except for the folks driving Harleys. For the most part, the older population drove those. I even knew a few motorcycle grandmas that roared into town every summer.

I slowed down as I passed the public beach. Lake Huron came into view with its pristine beaches. Not a wave in sight, and the sun shone overhead like a beacon. Charcoal grills fired up and the fragrance of cooking hot dogs wafted in the air, while seagulls overtook the picnic area, scavenging for food. Shrill shrieks from children at the playground pierced the air. Yes, summer has begun.

The downtown area would be overloaded with tourists browsing through gift shops and eating at Marion's Dairy Bar. That ice cream shop had been in business since 1945. It sported a sizable statue of a little boy holding an ice cream cone on its roof. Kinda reminded me of the Big Boy, but better. We also had a Dairy Queen in town, but there were many other places to find ice cream in East Tawas.

I pulled into Eleanor's gravel drive and noticed the house sported a fresh coat of white paint. It wasn't much to look at from the front except for a few windows and a door. Not even a hanging plant could be seen. She kept those on the deck. Eleanor also had a garage—painted white—and I hoped it contained her Cadillac. I'd hate to think she'd be driving to Walmart and running over some poor sap. Poor dear didn't have the best driving skills.

I opened her door, since sure enough, it wasn't locked. I'd given up on that argument. Eleanor wasn't the type to change anytime soon, except with the addition of her beau, Mr. Wilson. He's kinda decrepit and uses a walker, but at least Eleanor had somebody to cuddle with now and then. I can't be expected to entertain her all the time.

I had my own man, the hotshot lawyer Andrew Hart. He was also my former boss, but he was married back then. Who knew I'd reconnect with him at the age of seventy-two? We both were widowed, me at the age of forty-two. Life has been good since Andrew uttered the L-word, but I wished he were around more.

Eleanor and I were what you'd call senior snoops. We had even solved a cold case once. We had the great idea of starting a detective agency, but the paperwork still hadn't cleared. I'd blame the good Sheriff Peterson for that. I'm just sure he told the state how unsafe it was having old bags like us investigating crimes. He probably told them about how we interfered with his investigations—that we pulled our pink lady revolvers out too much. We handed them in at the recent police auction.

I wandered through Eleanor's house and froze when I saw something scuttle past me that was too big to be a mouse. I pressed myself against the kitchen cabinets as I panted out, "Eleanor!"

The screen to the patio door slid open and Eleanor's white-haired head stuck through it. She giggled, causing her curls to bounce and then pressed her plus-sized body through the rest of the way. Her belly was concealed under a white tee with the word 'Fuzzy's' in bright neon letters. Her yellow thongs poked out from under the white fuzzy pajama pants she wore.

"Aggie, what on earth?"

I clutched a fist over my heart. "I-I saw something scurry past me. Do you have rats?"

She frowned. "I sure hope not. What color was it?"

"I don't know," I gasped. "But it was big!"

Eleanor wrinkled up her pert nose and then her eyes widened. "Oh you must mean Mr. Tinkles."

"Mr. What?"

Just then a small dachshund came ambling toward Eleanor, who picked up the miniature version of the breed and rubbed it under its chin. Why, this dog was mud puddle brown.

He panted, and gave Eleanor a good licking. *Yuck* was all I could think.

"Stop it, Aggie, and be nice."

"Nice? It's a dog. I hope he's not yours."

She set the dog down, and it sat at El's feet. "Just because you hate dogs doesn't mean you have to be nasty about it. I need a pet too."

"I'm not being nasty. I'm just not a dog person." I tried to smile, but I just couldn't. "Eleanor, you can barely take care of yourself. Dogs are hard work."

"I know they are, but you have to admit he sure is a cutie."

Just then the pint-sized dog promptly trotted over, lifted a leg, and peed on my foot! "Oh God! Eleanor, he just peed on me!" I grabbed a paper towel and wet it with soap and water, then tried to wash the urine off both me and my sandal.

"I know. That's why his name is Mr. Tinkles."

I frowned. "Perfect name, but he's going to stink up your place with all that peeing."

She raised a finger into the air. "That's just the thing. He only pees on people he doesn't know. I think he's marking his territory."

"Well, he needs to mark it somewhere else. I hope you don't expect me to haul this pooch around with us."

"Well, we can some of the time. I just hate the thought of Mr. Tinkles being alone all day." She blinked at me. "We could take him with us to your place."

"I think not! Besides, Duchess hates dogs," I reminded her.

"I believe that was hell hounds, or one hell hound. Is Leotyne still at the campground?"

"Yes, but she moved across from me again. She might have mentioned that I needed to be protected."

El sauntered to her black and white plaid sofa and sat. "Protected from what?"

"Who knows, but I'm listening to her. She has yet to steer me wrong."

Eleanor drummed her fingers on her coffee table. "I like her, even if she's batshit crazy."

"That would sum up about all of us." I grimaced. "I mean that's what Sheriff Peterson would say about me."

"Did you hear—"

I cut in with, "I heard. Sheriff Peterson is now up for a re-election bid and I just don't know what to do?"

El shook her head. "No, I mean Hal Peterson has gone missing."

"Sheriff Peterson's dad?"

"Yup. The crotchety old man who was sprung from the County Medical Facility not long ago."

I pursed my lips. "Didn't he have a companion or something?"

"Yes, Raul something or other. He's long gone too."

"Well, maybe we should talk to Peterson and get the scoop. I can't imagine having his dad on the missing list would be good for the election, unless—"

"It's better for the election if he's on cold storage somewhere."

I motioned Eleanor up. "Come on then. We better get moving, daylights a wastin'."

She jumped up, grabbed her large black purse and tossed Mr. Tinkles inside.

"Oh no you're not," I insisted.

"We can drop him at your place on the way."

"No we can't. I don't want that flea bitten mutt in my camper."

Mr. Tinkles lifted his snout out and growled at me in response. "You hurt his feelings, Aggie."

"Fine, bring him along then, but I don't like it a bit!"

There was no sense in arguing with Eleanor because it would be a waste of breath. She did exactly what she wanted and only if she wanted. I love Eleanor dearly, but I'm not so sure what's going to happen when Duchess sees this pooch.

I gazed out the patio door as Eleanor closed it and put a metal rod in the track. It was blue sky and calm waters. I sure hoped it would go well with Peterson today. Lord knew the man can be impossible, but he had some hard questions to answer.

We walked out the front door and Eleanor ran to back her Caddy out of the garage. She zigzagged her way out, but did so without straying onto US 23 or running me over, so I was impressed. She hopped out and made her way into the passenger side, making herself comfortable inside. I slid behind the wheel and closed the door, staring at the blasted dog that I just wouldn't admit was kinda cute. His snout poked out and looked so sad that I had to pat his head. Mr. Tinkles responded by wagging his tail, which moved his whole body.

Chapter Two

Once we had settled in the Caddy with me at the helm, I backed up onto US 23 directly in front of Dorothy Alton's Buick. Brakes were screeched and horn was blasted, but I kept it moving. Dorothy was Eleanor's nemesis, so no sense in stopping and listening to a bunch of veiled threats thrown about. I had to question Sheriff Peterson.

I dropped Mr. Tinkles off at my camper and Duchesses' pupils grew big when we did. I imagine the poor dear didn't know what to think as she ran for cover, but there was no time to stay while they got acquainted. El and I had to try and catch Peterson before he trekked off to parts unknown.

I made it to the sheriff's department in record time and caught Peterson leaving. He was heading out to his car. I jerked to a stop and I made my way over to him as he sat in his cruiser. "Excuse me, Peterson. I need to talk to you," I said, as I rapped on his window.

"We have questions, you mean, Aggie," El piped up.

He unrolled his window a crack. "What is it this time? Another dead body with your name written all over it?"

I gripped the window with my fingers. "No, I heard your father Hal has turned up missing. Is that true?"

He unrolled the window more and promptly removed my fingers. "Let's just say for arguments sake it is. What then?"

"I'd like to question you about it is all. It must be a distraction with you up for re-election and Hal missing is all."

The sheriff swiped a hand over his sweat-dampened, dark hair. His tan tie had a visible mustard stain. The buttons of his brown sheriff's shirt strained and were nearly unable to contain his many rolls, which he had accumulated by too many donuts from Tim Horton's, no doubt. He was the most unfit sheriff yet.

After a lengthy pause, he said, "I have no idea where my dad is."

I pushed a stray lock of my hair back. "I thought you hired a companion for him?"

"I did."

"What's his name again?"

"It's Raul," Eleanor interjected.

I glared at her. "Would you let the sheriff answer, El!"

She folded her arms across her chest. "I was just trying to help!"

"Does this Raul have a last name?"

Peterson's face turned beet red. "I'm the sheriff and unless I missed something you two are not the law."

"I know, but perhaps we can be of some help here. Unless of course, you stashed your dad somewhere."

He narrowed his eyes, slapping on a pair of mirrored sunglasses. "Why would I do that?"

"So the old man can't make you look bad and hurt your political aspirations, for one."

El slapped her knee and laughed. "Just because the man pees in public doesn't mean he'd hurt Peterson's chances of re-election."

I grinned. "Then there are the hookers."

Peterson raised a brow. "Hookers! Have you taken leave of your senses?"

I straightened up and thought for a moment and then shot back with, "No, I don't think I have."

"Well, he called us hookers, Aggie."

"I know, and that couldn't be further from the truth."

"Of course not," El agreed. "You give it away for free."

"Are you two through? I don't have all day to yap like you two."

I should have been offended but I considered the source. "Just a few more questions if you please. Raul's last name is?"

"Perez."

"That's not very Cuban sounding," El pointed out. "It sounds Mexican."

"Hispanic," I corrected her. "The year is 2013, dear."

"I get so messed up with everything. I hate all this political correctness."

Peterson started his car and it rolled back as I asked, "Did you file a missing person's report?"

"No, he's just run off. I'm sure he'll be back when he runs out of money."

I frowned. "Doesn't he have dementia or something?"

"Yeah," El said. "It can't be safe for the old coot to be running around. He might get hurt."

"Or at least find another way to ruin the election," I fired back.

I moved out of the way as Peterson backed out and I hollered, "Don't worry, El and I are on the case!"

Peterson sped away.

"Do you think he heard us?" I asked El.

"I'm not sure, Aggie, but he flipped us the bird."

"He did not!"

"Maybe you need to get your eyes checked, dear."

"Well... he better not let me see it or he'll have the toughest election bid in the history of East Tawas!"

El patted my hand. "Calm down. Don't let the man rile you so."

"You'd think he'd be happy we are on the case."

El blinked. "Since when has Peterson ever been happy with anything we've done?"

"Good point. I bet he'll change his tune when we find his father."

"Poppycock. He doesn't want him found, is my thinking."

"I believe you're right, El. I wonder if Hal is still seeing Mildred Winfree."

"Beats me, but they have been hot and heavy since our ghost case."

I laughed. "She'd be a good person to question if she wasn't my nemesis."

"Well, that's true, but we have to at least try."

"Unless they're both missing."

"Might be. Maybe they ran off to get hitched."

I laughed. "They certainly are both nuts enough to, but somehow I can't see it." Truth was I couldn't see what ole Hal saw in Mildred. She's a shrew and vindictive. "She's definitely on our list. Do you know where we can find her, El?"

"Have to ask her sister, Elsie Bradford."

I winced at that. Ever since Mildred showed up in town I have been on the outs with Elsie. "Why would the woman give me the time of day?"

"You, Agnes Barton, need to get off your high horse. Elsie is still our friend, even though I body slammed Mildred not long ago. The sooner you two patch things up the better. Plus, she has some great card parties."

"I know, but what if... "

El rolled her eyes. "What if she throws you out the door... what if she shuns you? Life if full of what ifs and you can't let that stop you."

"Of course you're right. I might as well bite the bullet." I lightened up. "I heard they are having a craft show in town and I'm sure Elsie will be there."

El popped a glance at the sky overhead. "It's hot out here. Let's get back in the car and sort this out."

Once we were seated, I couldn't help but notice Trooper Sales pulling in and I watched until he disappeared in the sheriff's department. Obviously he was there for a reason, but what?

"Aggie, whatever are you looking at?"

I pointed to the trooper's cruiser. "Look who's here! Trooper Sales."

"And your point is?"

"I wonder why he's here?"

El threw her hands up. "How would I know? And I'm pretty sure he won't tell us."

"We'll have to head on over to Sophia's. Perhaps she has the scoop." I had yet to spend any quality time with Sophia since I came home from Florida and found out that ole Trooper Sales had gotten my granddaughter pregnant. It was bad enough when they were dating, but now, it would take all my restraint not to wring Trooper Sales' neck! The truth was, I liked Sales. He's a fair trooper and has always run a buffer between Sheriff Peterson and I. Lord knew on any given day the ole sheriff sure could put a wrench in my plans to investigate. As it stood, I didn't currently have a case, but things had a habit of changing in East Tawas. So Peterson's father was missing, eh? Did it have anything to do with the upcoming election? Would Peterson really stash his father somewhere until the election was over?

El tapped her fingers on the dash, "So, Sophia is in the family way, huh?"

I gripped the steering wheel in a death-like grip. "Yes."

"Do you think Trooper Sales is gonna step up to the plate?"

"He had better or I can't say what I'll do." Shotgun wedding came to mind. "Lord knows I can't count on my daughter, Martha, to put a plan into action."

Eleanor giggled. "Plan? Just what do you have cooped up in that head of yours?"

"Trooper Sales needs to marry my granddaughter, or else."

"Or else what? People don't have shotgun weddings anymore."

"We'll see."

"She might not even want to marry him. It's not like a single girl can't have a baby these days."

"I don't expect you to understand, but you do know how much I love my granddaughter."

"I know. She's been through a lot, but seriously, Agnes. You can't run the girls life." She paused. "So what's up with Martha?"

"Nothing besides getting under my skin." I changed the subject—anything to get my mind off the fact that my long lost daughter had returned to town and I was forced to let her stay with me. It's not like I could throw her out in the streets. "I'm still waiting for the go-ahead to move into my house. I have half a mind to call my insurance agent. There has to be some reason there's been a delay." It still bugged me that my house had been firebombed on a previous case.

"Don't worry, Agnes. I'm sure your house will be finished before the summer is up."

I made the turn down Sophia's driveway and screeched to a stop. Sophia was standing outside with a strange man who was dressed in a blue suit and tie. I had to put a hand over my eyes for a moment to cut the shiny reflection coming off the man's shoes!

"Hello there," the man greeted us, shoving a flyer into our palms. "I'm Clay Barry. I'm running for Iosco County Sheriff."

I surveyed the candidate before me. His dark hair was slicked back and he had trim hips, unlike the burgeoning frame of Sheriff Peterson. He was quite attractive, with rugged good looks and piercing brown eyes.

Finally I said, "And where do you hail from?"

"I have been a deputy in Redwater, Michigan, for ten years. That's in the thumb of Michigan."

"I can't say I have ever heard of Redwater before."

"Me either," Eleanor interjected. "It sounds made up to me."

Clay hugged the stack of flyers close to his frame. "I hear that all the time, but Redwater isn't much different than East Tawas. It's also on Lake Huron."

"I'm perfectly aware of what lake borders the thumb of Michigan, young man. How old are you?"

"Jeez, Aggie. I thought you'd like a younger sheriff in town."

"Who says I want a change in guard? I like Sheriff Peterson just fine."

El laughed. "Seriously?"

"I'm thirty-two and an experienced law enforcement man. You should come to my fundraiser later today and learn more about me. My mother is even going to be there."

His mother, really? "I might just do that. Where is it?"

"At the East Tawas public beach."

I nodded as Clay walked away, putting a flyer on the cars of the neighbors who didn't answer their doors.

"Well, it looks like ole Peterson has some stiff competition."

"He sure is a handsome fella," El put in.

Sophia stood watching El and I.

I finally said, "Let's go inside. I have had enough excitement for the day."

We followed Sophia inside and noticed her place was in complete disarray, with boxes trailing from her kitchen to the bedroom. Each of them had been etched in black marker.

My heart thudded against my chest. "Are you moving?"

Sophia smiled, her cheeks rosy. She adjusted her wavy hair's ponytail holder. She was dressed in denim shorts and white tee, pink flip-flops on her feet. "Yes, I wanted to tell you before, but ever since you came back from Florida you have been so busy."

Nothing like stalling, I thought. "Go on."

"Isn't it obvious?" El spat.

"No, it's not obvious to me," I retorted.

"You're moving in with Bill, aren't you?" El asked with a wink.

I grabbed my throat when Sophia nodded. "What—ttt?"

Sophia put her hands up in a defensive mode. "Don't go all granny on me. I'm pregnant and moving in with Bill. It's the next step."

"No, getting married is the next step. You skipped one."

"Oh, Gramms. You don't have to get married these days just because you're pregnant."

"Yes, you do. Do you realize what the gossip mongers will do if you don't?"

Everyone looked at El until she muttered. "What?"

"You can't keep a secret if you tried."

"Well, Sophia won't be able to keep this secret too much longer," El said. "You should both know I'm not going to say a word, but this is a small town and people talk in a small town."

"They had better not let me hear them say anything about my Sophia." I hugged Sophia. "I hope you know what you're doing, dear, but did Bill at least ask you to marry him?"

"No, and I want you to stay out of it. I don't want Bill to feel railroaded into popping the question. It won't mean anything if he only does it because you made him feel like he had to. So keep your shotgun unloaded."

"And what about your mother?"

"You should know how Martha is, Gramms. We're still trying to mend our relationship."

I gave Sophia one last parting hug and made my way back to the car. Once Eleanor settled herself I took off down the road with a rumble, a smoke trail in my wake.

Chapter Three

I parked the caddy on the main drag, and El and I jaywalked across US 23. Tables were lined on the streets, hawking a variety of crafts.

"How are we going to find Elsie?" I asked El.

El pointed ahead of us. "Let's ask Rosa Lee Hill."

Rosa Lee Hill had quite the crowd and I knew why when I spotted the brownies. We made our way to her side. "I hope those aren't the same brownies. You know, the ones with the special ingredient." How else was I supposed to ask her if the brownies contained marijuana by-product?

She wiped a hand over her green sleeveless blouse. "Don't be silly. The sheriff has already been by to check."

"He just wants to make sure you retired from the medicinal business for good."

She tucked her thin hair behind each ear. "I grow plants for potpourri these days. I have a nice shop where Roy's Bait and Tackle used to be. You should stop by sometime."

Rosa Lee picked out purple and pink flowers, exchanging them for a twenty from a lady with a purple dress. "Make sure you get these into water when you get home," she informed the woman.

I stared at the incense displayed in glass jars. There were some pretty intense fragrances here, not unlike being at a flower shop. I sniffled a little at the perfumed sticks that smelled worse than a perfume factory.

"Have you seen Elsie Bradford?"

"Sure, she's right over there."

I followed where Rosa Lee pointed out. Elsie stood out, dressed in her powder blue ensemble like always. We thanked Rosa Lee for the info and made tracks toward Elsie, who was selling cloth dolls, each with a painted canvas face.

Elsie looked up when she spotted us, but continued to sell dolls to a group of young women who wore matching blue bikinis.

"Hello, Elsie," I finally said.

"You're back from Florida I see. You could have at least said goodbye first," she huffed.

Was Elsie mad because we didn't say goodbye, for real? "Well, I guess I didn't know you cared."

"It's the least you could do. We are friends, after all."

"We are? But I thought you were mad at me because of Mildred."

She pursed her lips, which widened her cheeks. "Don't be silly. I know how Mildred can get. It's all ancient history between you two. I was shocked when my sister hit you like that."

I searched the crowd. "Where is Mildred?"

"Oh I don't know. Ever since she met Hal Peterson she hasn't been very reliable. She was supposed to help me sell these dolls."

I glanced at one particular doll with a hideous expression on its face. "She must have helped you make a few dolls, at least."

She stared at the doll I was just looking at. "Sure, but she's not very artistic."

"When was the last time you saw her?"

"About a week ago, why?"

"Well, I heard Hal Peterson is missing."

"Oh my! If he's missing, then so is my sister."

"So you think they were together when they disappeared?"

Elsie nodded. "I'm sure of it. What do you think happened to them? I mean in your expert sleuth opinion?"

"Well, they might have just taken a trip, but Hal has a companion, Raul Perez. If anything, they are all together somewhere. I had wondered if it has anything to do with the upcoming election."

"True, Hal certainly is an embarrassment to Sheriff Peterson. The last time he was over, he peed in my indoor tree's pot."

I stifled a giggle. "Oh my."

"There's no talking to Mildred about it though. She's fallen for Hal pretty hard."

"Wow, I just don't understand that one. I had always thought Mildred hated men."

"Me too, after her divorce that is, but it seems she's forgotten all about that." Elsie's eyes pled with me. "Please find my sister. I'd be happy to pay for your trip. I remember my sister mentioning that she and Hal might go to the casino sometime."

"Thanks, Elsie. That's a good tip, but did she mention which one?"

"Mt. Pleasant I believe."

"Thanks!"

El and I gave Elsie a quick hug and we left. From the way her eyes bulged out, you'd have thought she'd much prefer to be a comfortable distance from us. I was happy for a few reasons; Elsie really wasn't mad at me and I found out where her sister and Hal Peterson might have gone.

"So we're heading to Mt. Pleasant?" El asked as she rubbed her hands together.

"Not yet we're not. I want to check out the fundraiser for the new candidate. He said his mother would be there. You can tell a lot about someone from meeting their mother."

El snickered. "I wonder what people think when they meet you."

"I can't be blamed with how Martha turned out."

"She's your mirror image if you ask me."

I gasped. "I don't gallivant around in cat suits."

"No, but you do shop at Victoria Secret for undies."

"What do you expect me to wear, granny panties?"

"No, but they do sell bikini briefs at Walmart, you know."

"I know that, but I like going to Saginaw once in a while."

"Is that right. Then why haven't we been there recently?"

"Because none of our cases have led us there, smarty pants!"

"I could go for some real shopping at a real mall for a change. Sometimes I wish East Tawas had more places to shop at."

"I know, but we have so many quaint shops. You just can't get that anywhere else."

We drove to the East Tawas public beach and there was already quite the crowd. Red and blue streamers hung off a small stage and they were selling hotdogs and soda from stands.

An older woman, dressed snugly in a lavender dress, stood shoving a hot dog into her mouth while clutching a beer can, and it was all I could do not to shout, "You can't do that at the beach." From what I was aware, you can't even drink beer in public like that outside unless it's at bar patio or beer tent.

I strode up to the woman as she chomped on her hotdog and waited until she was done. I then said, "You do know you can't drink beer at the public beach."

Her cheeks became fire engine red. "Did my son send you over here?"

I shrugged. "I don't think I know your son. Is he someone special?"

"Well, he is running for sheriff in this county."

I gasped. "Really? So you must be Clay Barry's mother. I met him earlier and he told me his mother would be here."

"Undoubtedly. I'm Mrs. Barry."

El leaned forward on her toes. "Do you have a first name?"

"Yes, but everybody calls me Mrs. Barry so you can too."

I smiled. "That's awfully formal for someone drinking beer on the beach. If you keep that kind of business up, you'll make Sheriff Peterson happy."

"My son is a shoe-in for sheriff. As you can see, my son is very fit and much younger than that rot gut Peterson."

I felt offended, like I had to stick up for Peterson. "He's a good sheriff. I can't imagine any newcomer would stand a chance against him."

"Well, you're wrong there. My son is going to clean up this town."

"East Tawas is already cleaned up and nicer than you'll find anywhere in Michigan."

"Redwater is a nice town too."

"Then why isn't he running for sheriff there?"

"Be-because, my dear lady, he wants to run here."

I rolled my eyes just as the sheriff's car rolled into the parking lot. His car screeched to a stop and he rumbled out, making tracks toward us. Eying the beer can, his face reddened. "There's no beer allowed on the beach. Can't you read the sign?" he bellowed.

"I can read just fine. I'll throw it away if it bothers all you people so much," an exasperated Mrs. Barry said.

"So what gives, Peterson? Fancy meeting you here," I said.

He eyed up the banner and replied, "I received a few complaints, but I'll take my leave since it's settled." At that he left—obviously not wanting to interfere in the fundraiser of his opponent.

A black sedan drove up and I shuddered momentarily. Ever since goons had shot at El and me during a case, black sedans gave me the willies.

Clay Barry exited the sedan, followed by two comical looking senior ladies who were dressed alike, in white leggings underneath yellow shirts displaying a large Macaw dead center that was done in blue, red, and green vibrant sequins. It was hideous. It looked worse than what I had seen earlier at the craft show. Both ladies had pinched faces with bright rouge applied to their cheekbones. Their hair was swooped up into a beehive of sorts, and who wore one of those these days? It dated back to the 60's when women had their hair done once a week by beauticians of the day.

Eleanor shuddered in shock. "Would you look at that?"

"I'm seeing but I'm not believing."

"Well, believe it all right, girls," came the voice of Mrs. Barry behind them. "Those are the bird sisters, Mrs. Peacock and Mrs. Canary." She went on further to explain. "Mrs. Peacock has a Macaw. Strange bird talks more than most folks I know. Real insightful."

"I see," I muttered between snickers. "Your son sure has his supporters, but dear... are any of them residents of East Tawas?"

"Well, no," Mrs. Barry admitted. "They're here to rally support."

"Hopefully they left the beer in the car. I'd hate to see more beer on the beach."

Mrs. Barry's faced reddened. "Nothing wrong with a little beverage on the beach. You folks here in East Tawas are mighty fussy."

"We're decent folks, you mean."

Mrs. Barry greeted the bird sisters and glared at us, as did the sisters. Obviously she had shared her dislike for El and I.

I whispered to El. "I for one wasn't about to let this Clay Barry win the election. I mean what if his mother moved to town?"

"It would get mighty lively around here real quick-like."

"There's nothing wrong with a little booze, but there is a place and time."

"Yah, like Elsie's card parties," El said with a wink.

I'd rather not venture as to what Eleanor was referring to. Truth be known, it had been a long time since we had attended what used to be the event of the week. Elsie's parties were always a doctor's worse nightmare. There were enough fatty and salty treats to clog everyone's arteries that attended, not to mention spiked lemonade. They were the best parties, ever.

Clay gave his a mom a quick hug. "Isn't my son a looker?" Mrs. Barry asked.

"I wonder where he got his good looks from."

"Obviously his father," El said with a snicker, gaining her a cold look from the Barry group.

"My son is going to be the next Iosco County Sheriff come election time," Mrs. Barry insisted.

"Thanks mom," Clay said with a nod. "I sure hope so. It shouldn't be too hard to win, what with Peterson's record."

I put a finger in the air. "What do you mean, 'record'?"

He looked away for a moment and then locked eyes with me. "Well, allowing you and your friend there to interfere in investigations." He cleared his throat as El gasped. "No offense meant to you ladies, but you're not even private investigators from what I gathered. Not officially anyway. Yet Peterson has allowed you onto crime scenes and to help with investigations. Don't let me get started about what Trooper Sales has allowed you to do. He should have been suspended for allowing you to overlook case files on the Robinson's cold case murders."

I squared my shoulders. How could this man know so much about El and I or our activities in and around East Tawas? I smelled a rat. Had a trooper or deputy spilled the beans? Yet, he had it all wrong. "For one thing. I just received my PI license in the mail this morning," I lied. Well, it was supposed to be coming back any day now. Peterson even sent a letter of recommendation. "Neither Sheriff Peterson or Trooper Sales allowed us at crime scenes. We either were the ones to discover the bodies or were called to the scene of the crime by worried citizens."

"Yeah!" El spouted. "He even locked us up once when we interfered."

I nodded curtly. "If that's your whole platform you might as well go back to Hell, Michigan, where you came from."

"Redwater," Mrs. Barry yelled. "We're from Redwater."

"Go back there then. I'm sure he'd stand a better chance at becoming a sheriff there," El added.

Mrs. Barry's fist flew forward and caught Eleanor right under the chin. El flew to the ground with a thump, her body swaying with the impact. I then grabbed Mrs. Barry's shoulders and gave her a shake, rattling her head, I hope. How dare she hit Eleanor that way? If anything, I was the one who had spouted off the most.

The bird ladies came forward with claws raised and scratched my arms. I let out a howl, but by then El was back on her feet and she swung her purse at Mrs. Peacock, connecting with her cheek. She went down and El kicked sand in her eyes. Screams and howls echoed from us all as we each inflicted injury on the others until cop cars could be heard in the background.

"Shit, the coppers are coming," El shouted at she gripped my arm.

Sheriff Peterson exited his car almost before it completely came to a stop. He yanked at his waistband as he asked, "What's going on here?"

Clay pointed a bony finger in my face. "These ladies attacked my mother and her friends."

El and I searched the ground and sure enough all three ladies from Redwater were on the ground. El was hunched over, but I was on my feet, in total control over my body, rubbing my hands over the scratch wounds I received from the bird sisters. "We... I didn't either. Mrs. Barry started it when she hit Eleanor."

Eleanor profusely nodded. "She did, Peterson. I swear."

Peterson looked from Mrs. Barry to the bird sisters and back to El and I. "In that case, I'm arresting all of you."

Clay's face reddened and he looked about ready to shoot smoke from his ears. "You aren't arresting my mom!"

"Sorry, but I am. I'm arresting Agnes and Eleanor too, so that should make you feel better. I'm not playing any favorites here."

Clay shook a fist in the air. "You'll be sorry for this, Peterson!"

Deputies came forward and cuffed the lot of us, and escorted us to waiting squad cars—making sure to place Mrs. Barry and the bird sisters into a separate one from El and I.

Eleanor was sniveling until I shot her a look. "Here we go again," I vented.

"I don't know why we were arrested. They started it."
"Don't worry. I'm sure we'll get sprung soon enough," I reassured El.

Chapter Four

When the squad cars rolled into the sheriff's department, newsmen were at the ready with a boom camera trained on the scene. The two stone-faced deputies all but ignored citizens who held out cell phones—taking pictures and video, undoubtedly. I might think the whole deal strange, but it's not every day there is a brawl at a political fundraiser. Then again, this was politics. It didn't help that El and I had a reputation for getting into mischief.

We were then led towards the back room where I knew from previous experience we would be processed. I almost shuddered at thinking about the upcoming strip search. To my surprise, they simply took our fingerprints and mug shots, escorting us afterward into a holding cell.

A large female deputy that was pressed into a tan uniform swung back the barred door and ordered us inside. "Look here. We only have one holding cell for women so I expect you all to behave yourselves."

El and I went to the right and sat down while the bird sisters and Mrs. Barry sat on the bench to the left.

Mrs. Peacock stared around the cell. "Well, they certainly could use a decorator in here."

"Yes, sister," Mrs. Canary replied. "Isn't it dreadful."

El choked out, "You do realize you're in jail and not the Hyatt, don't you, dear?"

Mrs. Barry puffed up her chest. "Which we wouldn't even be in if you and your friend hadn't showed up at my son's fundraiser."

I squeezed my hands together tightly, my nails digging into my palms. "You swung the first punch, Mrs. Barry."

"What was I supposed to do when you kept insinuating my son had no chance of winning the election?"

"Why should you be bothered by what I have to say? Elections can get pretty dirty sometimes. Maybe it would be best if you went home and let your son handle his own affairs."

"My son is not a cheater," Mrs. Barry insisted. "That Polly girl made up the whole story about my son."

That got El's attention. "Who's Polly?"

Mrs. Canary rubbed her hands together. "She's a woman Clay was reputed to be having an affair with."

"But it's not true," Mrs. Barry insisted. "She's lying. She has been trying to get with my son for some time, but he keeps rejecting her advances."

I smiled like a cat just then. "That's what they all say, dear." So Clay supposedly had an affair with this Polly lady. I wonder how many other secrets he was hiding.

Half an hour later, the iron-bar door flew open and the female deputy from earlier said, "You're all sprung. It seems Sheriff Peterson has had a change of heart and has decided not to charge you ladies."

"What about my Caddy?" El asked.

"You can pick it up from impound."

El narrowed her eyes. "That's just great! And I suppose I'll still have to pay the impound fee."

"Well, yes. You should know, Miss Eleanor, how it works. I imagine you saw that on an episode of CSI Miami."

I squeezed El's arm. "Don't worry. I'll pay the fine for you."

"I think Mrs. Barry should be the one to pay the fine. It was her fault we were arrested in the first place."

"Fat chance," Mrs. Barry spat as she walked down the hallway ahead of us.

When we rounded the counter of the main desk, Trooper Sales was there with my daughter Martha. Her slim body was contained beneath a jungle print cat suit, her long hair in total disarray like she had just gotten out of bed! She flashed her green eyes at me. "Well, Mother. What's the charge this time? Fight at the beach again?"

"Sort of," El volunteered. "We were attacked at a political fundraiser for Sheriff Peterson's opponent."

"Really? I'd have thought you two would be rallying for support for anyone running against ole Peterson. It's not like you like him all that much."

"I thought that, until his opponent, Clay Barry, told us he's using us against Peterson."

"He didn't actually say it that way, Aggie," El reminded me.

"No, but if you ask me this new candidate sounds way stricter than Peterson. What if this Clay is actually elected? He might stop us from investigating crimes in East Tawas," I pointed out.

El rubbed her knuckles. "He better not try or I'm gonna give him a one... two... three," she threatened.

"Seriously, El. We can't do anything like that to law enforcement, and even though I have been at odds with Peterson—I can't allow a man like that Clay character to be our new sheriff. We'd be sunk if that happens."

Martha rolled her eyes. "Oh boy. I never expected you to say something like that, but what can you do?"

"We can sway public opinion is what," I said with a wink. "Mrs. Barry said something about some Polly woman having an affair with Clay. That sounds like perfect dirt."

"She also said he rejected this Polly," El said with a bob of her head. "You had to have heard her say that, Aggie."

I sighed nosily. "Of course, El. We need to find this Polly and find out the scoop. Maybe she followed him to East Tawas."

"She could be a stalker," Martha said with a grin. She led the way toward her seventies station wagon. We squeezed ourselves into the backseat that was practically all covered with clothing. Martha all but lived in the car on occasion. For the time being, she was staying with me in my Winnebago. I just hoped by the time I was able to move back into my house that she'd find accommodations elsewhere.

As Martha adjusted the rear view mirror she asked, "Where to, mother?"

It grated on my nerves whenever Martha referred to me as mother. It wasn't so much the word as the tone when she said it. "Let's head back to my camper. I need to check and see if Eleanor's dog has torn up the place."

Martha cranked the engine and asked, "Since when does Eleanor have a dog?" Making the turn onto US 23, she veered in the direction of the campground.

I shrugged, and just then Eleanor chimed in. "He's a stray. Poor dear was panting up a storm."

Martha pulled on a pair of sunglasses and asked, "So he just showed up at your door?"

"Yes, and I had to let the poor thing inside for a bite to eat. Lord knows he needed a healthy drink of water."

I gripped the seat as Martha made a wild turn. "You should know you shouldn't let a stray in the house."

"Yah," Martha said. "Once you feed them you're stuck with them, or at least that's what happens with most of my dates."

My eyes widened. "You mean before you decided to crash at my place, right?"

She gripped the steering wheel. "Actually, I have this fella Pete that insists we're meant to be together. He just won't take a hint and shove off."

I grabbed my purse in a death-like grip. "Getting back to the dog. He has to have an owner somewhere, Eleanor. Maybe we should make up some lost and found posters."

"No way. I'm not about to give Mr. Tinkles away. Losers weepers, finders keepers!"

"Fine, I'll let it drop for now, but Eleanor, really? He could have a family out there somewhere that is frantically searching for him."

Eleanor pouted, just as Martha pulled into my spot at the East Tawas campground.

The campground was bustling with activity. Campers were trailing their way toward the pier with fishing poles in hand, while children scampered about, heading to the beach. It was promising to be a great day as the sun already beat down on us. I spotted Leotyne Williams across from my site, the same gypsy that rolled into town last summer. She wore a long black dress as always and had a pipe clenched between her teeth. I waved and she simply nodded. I guess I should be happy enough with that. Truth be known, that woman gave me the willies. She was cooking something over an open fire that smelled putrid. I hoped it wasn't anyone I knew. Sure, we had gotten along much better, but there was something about that woman that rattled me. Folks might think it a mite strange to be scared of a gypsy these days, but I can't help how I feel. Maybe it was her sunken eyes. She looks like she recently crawled out of the grave. The movie Drag Me Back to Hell came to mind.

We clamored out of the car and I reached for the door handle, listening intently. There wasn't a sound to speak of. Had Duchess eaten Mr. Tinkles? I opened the door expecting carnage of sorts. Possibly entrails strewn across my trailer, maybe my cat had eaten the tiny dog whole! I had not expected to see what I did, which was Mr. Tinkles nestled next to my cat, Duchess, and that she was licking him enthusiastically!

"Well, I'll be—"

"You'll be a monkey's uncle, Aggie?"

I gave her a sharp look, knelt and gave the small dog a pat while Duchess lazily gazed toward me. That was until the yapping started. The dog ambled onto its small legs, its pointy nose near my ankle as he proceeded to bark up a storm. "What's your deal pooch?"

"He can tell you're a dog hater," El said with a chuckle.

"I am not. They are just too high maintenance."

"Oh and Duchess isn't? Didn't you say you give her a can of tuna a day?"

I made tracks for the door and opened it, yelling at Mr. Tinkles, "Out."

"You can't just let him out there without a leash," El spat. "He might run away."

"Hopefully back to where he came from."

El scooped up the dog and asked, "Don't you have a leash for Duchess?"

I opened a drawer and pulled out the pink leash that Duchess wanted no part of, handed it to Eleanor and waited until she took the dog outside. When she returned, I suggested, "Maybe we can get back to business now."

"Meaning what, Aggie?"

"Just that we need to find Hal Peterson."

El's eyes widened. "Really? We're really going to the casino?"

"Yes, that is, if Martha swings by the impound yard so we can get your Cadillac."

Martha flopped into a nearby chair and said, "Why not take my wagon?"

I frowned. "For one, I have no clue if it will make the trip without clunking out."

Trouble in Tawas

"It's a sound car, Mother."

"What year is it anyway?"

"Nineteen seventy something, but I swear to you that I haven't had a lick of trouble with it. I really don't feel like going anywhere right now." She stretched. "I need a nap."

"Great idea," El said. "Me too."

I took Martha's keys. "You can sleep on the way, Eleanor."

We crawled back into the station wagon, and when we'd settled ourselves, Eleanor cranked on the radio, but only static blared from the speakers. I turned a knob and frowned as a political ad came on promoting Clay. He's gonna clean up East Tawas, whatever in the hang that meant, and not allow any interference with investigations. I think that meant El and I.

"Does she have any tapes?" El asked.

I stared at the radio and asked, "You mean 8-track tapes, dear?"

El giggled. "Wow, this car sure is old."

"But not as old as us," I pointed out. "Look in that box on the floor board."

El opened it and the aroma of marijuana about blew us over. "Wow, smells like good shit."

"Close it before the whole car reeks." I didn't feel good about going anywhere with that stuff in the car. "So no 8-track tapes down there?"

El came back with an Elton John tape and inserted it into the player just as we rolled down the road, making our way onto US 23. Soon El was snoozing up a storm, obviously more tired than I thought, but us older folks can often nod off quite easily once we get into a comfy position.

Chapter Five

Hours later, I drove under the huge Soaring Eagle Casino and Resort sign, with two bald eagles on either side of the sign. I could see they went to great expense to attract gamblers from across the state. Sure, there were other Indian-run casinos in Michigan, but this one ranked as my favorite. I had won a spot of money now and then, but overall I about lost my shirt, I chuckled to myself.

As I pulled in front of the casino I nudged El, who popped awake. "What? Where?"

"We're here," I told her as I got out of the car, accepting the ticket given to me by the wide-eyed valet upon seeing our mode of transportation. Sure enough, all eyes were on us and our out-of-place wagon. I rounded the car, met Eleanor on the sidewalk and shrugged. "I don't see what the hoopla is."

"It's not every day you see a vintage ride like Martha's wagon."

El and I linked arms and made our way through the double doors. Bells, whistles, and vibrations hit us like a wave. Security guards stared us down, then shifting their eyes toward the right where a line had formed where you get your membership cards. You simply have only to put them in machines to accumulate credits, which are then uploaded onto the cards.

I observed the crowd carefully and then asked El, "Is this a hospital, or casino?" How could I not think that, when the place was loaded with senior citizens with canes, walkers, and wheelchairs—even some rolling portable oxygen tanks behind them.

"I had no idea there were that many people our age that gambled."

"Yeah, like if they ever hit a jackpot, they'd probably keel over from a heart attack."

El giggled. "How right you are." A strange look came over El's face and she announced, "I hafeta pee."

After we both used the bathroom, we stood washing our hands

under the automatic faucets and El asked, "How in the heck are we gonna find Mildred and Hal?"

"Let's just browse for a while. Maybe we'll get lucky."

"I have a twenty. I'm gonna play something."

"That's not why we're here, Eleanor."

"Geez I know that, but why not?"

"Because you'll just lose your money is why not?"

Eleanor made her way to the counter to ask for quarters, only to be told that she just had to insert the bills directly into the machine. "I liked it much better the other way," El told me. "I loved carrying around a bucket of quarters. I just loved hearing them rattle together."

"With your ears, dear?"

"I can hear just fine if you need to know."

"That's a good thing to know." I grimaced. I should have known better than to mention that Eleanor sometimes couldn't hear at times, but then again, we are senior citizens. It's to be expected.

El stopped in front of a Lucky 7 machine and put her twenty in. Credits counted up, and she played for ten minutes before she lost all her money. I couldn't hold myself back. "Told you so."

"Oh phooey. You gave me bad luck."

"What a thing to say. I thought we were pretty good together."

"Sleuthing, we are. Why not search for Hal yourself while I try another twenty."

I put my foot down. "No way. I'll lose you for sure."

Eleanor pouted but followed me despite how I knew she felt. *She's thinking I'm a fun sucker like usual*, I thought.

After a half hour of going down rows and rows of slot machines, I threw my arms up. "I give up. We'll never find them!"

"Why not just page him, dear?" Eleanor suggested. "That is, if they can hear over the roar in here."

"Good idea, Eleanor. I knew I brought you with me for a reason."

"Like you could ever go it alone."

I nodded as we made our way to the counter and asked them to page Hal Peterson. The announcer said, "Hal Peterson, your party is waiting for you."

I searched the crowd and nearly gave up when a bright-eyed Hal surfaced, one hand under his red suspenders that held up his brown trousers. The white tee shirt he wore underneath was stained with ketchup and I figured that's why we never ran across him before. I bet he was having lunch.

Hal's eyes narrowed as he spied us, "Where's the party? I'm so ready to party," he exclaimed as he danced around, or shuffled his feet.

"It's back in East Tawas," I suggested.

"I'm not going back there. I'm not out of money yet."

I glanced behind him. "Where is Raul?"

He scratched his big belly. "Who?"

"Your companion."

"Beats me, back to Mexico for all I know." He whispered to me, "I think he's an illegal."

I shook my head. "I have a hard time believing your son would hire an illegal to watch over you."

"Humph, that harebrained son of mine doesn't know his head from his shinola."

"He's worried about you," I lied. Truth was, it was important for me to get ole Hal back in town.

He snapped his false teeth out and proceeded to clean them with his shirt. "You sure are touched in the head if you believe that line of bull. He'd take me back to the old folk's home for sure if he gets ahold of me."

Eleanor butted in. "But he took you out of that place."

"Sure he did, but I know he didn't want to. Kept grumbling about my behavior." He stopped talking to blow his nose on a red hanky he'd pulled from his pocket, before continuing, "He thinks his own father is an embarrassment."

"Well, that's just awful." El glanced toward me and added, "I know exactly how you feel."

Hal licked his lips, staring at El's ample bosom. "Hey, are you still with Mr. Wilson?"

"Of course. He makes the best tuna casserole in all of Michigan."

"I see, well... if you break up, I have a twenty with your name on it," he suggested.

"Twenty!" El shouted. "What on earth are you talking about?"

"You two are hookers, right?"

I rolled my eyes. "Not that I'm aware of. Neither Eleanor nor I have ever worked as hookers."

El gave me a sheepish look, but remained silent. "Besides, you're seeing Mildred Winfree, aren't you?"

"What if I am? A man is allowed to date more than one woman if he wants to these days."

"Not unless he wants a black eye," El spat.

I interrupted them before this got out of hand. "By the way, where is Mildred?"

"She went to the spa."

"She needs it too," I blurted out before I thought.

"Be nice Agnes, she's your nemesis, not a troll," El said.

"You could use a trip yourself," Hal told me.

I winced at that, but I deserved the barb. Lord knows I hardly even put on makeup these days. "You, on the other hand, are a picture of what an older man should be, right?"

He rubbed his belly. "I sure am. I have plenty of ladies eyeing me up today, too."

"Exactly how much money are you putting in those machines?" El asked.

"Oh I don't know. I've lost track." He paused and then added, "Whatever the card holds, I suppose."

"Whose money are you spending?"

"Raul gave me his credit card for safe keeping."

What in the hell? "That's about the dumbest thing I have ever heard. He actually gave you the card, or you took it?"

"He never took anything," a freshly made up Mildred spat as she walked up. Her high silver hair made her look like Frankenstein's bride. "Raul must have gave it to Hal, right sweetie?"

"Well, his wallet was there and I was sure he wouldn't mind if I borrowed his card. I planned to pay him back when I won."

"If you won, you mean. We better head back to East Tawas before you lose any more of his money."

"It's not his money, it's the credit card company's money," Mildred said in a sour tone.

"It's only a credit line, Mildred. Raul will be responsible for all the money you spent."

"Did you at least win a little back?" Eleanor asked.

"Not so far, but I have a feeling I'm about to. Maybe I would have by now if you hookers hadn't interrupted me when I was on a roll."

Mildred spoke up. "You didn't leave the credits in the machine, I hope."

He pulled a slip from his pocket. "Nope, I'm not an idiot, woman."

I took the slip from him that read 'fifty cents'. "Wow, what a roll. How about rolling with us back to East Tawas."

"Not until I win more money."

"That's not your card. You're stealing Raul's money. I'm sure he won't be too happy when he finds out."

Hal frowned and darted to the right, disappearing into a crowd of eager gamblers. I moved into action and pursued him with El hot on my heels.

"What is the hay?" El shouted. "How did we lose him so quick?"

"We need to keep moving. We have to find him before he gets into trouble."

"Which he already kinda is."

An hour later El and I flopped down onto a bench, exhausted. "I h-have no idea what to do next."

"How about home?" El suggested. "I'm so tired and starving."

"I'll book a room for us and we can look for Hal later. How far could he have gone?"

"I don't know, but this sure is a big place."

El and I ate dinner at the casino's buffet and my jaw about slacked open when I found out what it would cost me for a room. I shelled out the two hundred dollars and when we entered our suite, I was both shocked and awed. It was a one bedroom suite with fireplace and sunken tub Jacuzzi. I sank down on the tan plush comforter covering the bed and practically melted. This was great. I made a quick call to let Martha know we wouldn't be coming home tonight. I also asked her to check out if anyone by the name of Polly had recently come to East Tawas. I then explained to her how this Polly might be having an affair with Clay Barry and how it might help Peterson out if we could find her.

When I hung up the phone, El announced, "I want to get in the Jacuzzi."

"I'm not sure who is gonna help you get out."

El shucked her clothes and I glanced away as she filled the tub and climbed in. The water rolled to the surface and El giggled like a school girl. "Now this is what I call relaxing. Jump in, Agnes."

Hands went to my hips. "I will not!"

"What are you afraid of, a little fun?"

Thinking about both El and I naked in the tub together I nodded. "Yup, that's it."

Sure enough, a half hour later I went to the tub and took ahold of El's hand to try and assist her from the tub. Her hand slipped... she gripped me harder and—I fell headlong into the tub. I bumped into Eleanor who squealed in delight. "It's about time, old girl."

I righted myself and made as dignified a retreat as I could, crawling out. Eleanor clamored out also and stared at my clothes. "What you gonna do now? It's not like you have a spare set of clothes."

I changed and donned a white bathrobe. "I'm sure there is some kind of shop here where I can buy something else to wear in this hotel."

We wandered back to the casino, where we were told there was a gift shop. I wasn't about to be bothered by the strange stares I received, either. At this point I had no dignity left. If I have learned anything in our adventures, it was to roll with the flow. It won't be the last time I'm caught in an awkward position.

I bought pink sweat pants and a Soaring Eagle tee, and took them back to my room. En route, I receive a few wolf whistles from college kids we passed in the hallway. "Way to go Grandma," a boy shouted. "You're way cooler than my grandma."

I nodded and slipped into our room, quick like. At this moment all I wanted to do was crawl into bed and get some sleep, which is just what I did.

Chapter Six

I awoke to a smiling Eleanor who held a ceramic coffee cup in her hands. "About time you woke up, sleepy head."

I slid my feet out of the covers and took the offered coffee. "Thanks, Eleanor. I slept like the dead."

"I know. I had to take your pulse to see if you were still kicking." She handed me my clothes. "So, what's in store for our adventures today?"

"I'm showering and we're heading back home. There's no case with Hal. He's obviously not missing."

"What about him having Raul's credit card?"

I ran my fingers through my hair in an attempt to straighten it. "That's his problem, not mine. I have bigger fish to fry."

"Or possibly his son's problem if charges get pressed."

I couldn't imagine what ole Sheriff Peterson would do if that happened. It might even hurt the election. "Let's just hope that won't happen."

"And by fish to fry, you mean?"

"Help Sheriff Peterson win this election."

"That's a switch, but I'm with you on that one. At least we don't have a murderer on our hands."

I shuddered like someone had just walked on my grave. "Don't say that, El. Every time you say that something dreadful happens."

"Shucks, don't blame me. People in town just drop off sometimes."

"Not without help they don't, except for the ones that die of natural causes."

***

After I showered, El and I placed our belongings in a bag from the hotel. It sure was heavy though, and I had to take out the towels. "El, we can't take the towels or we'll be charged." It was then I glanced at the mini bar. "Put that alcohol back!"

El frowned but did as she was told. When we strode out to get our car from the valet, Hal and Mildred were sitting on the curb.

"So what gives?" I asked the pair.

Hal shrugged. "Out of money. That damn Raul couldn't have had a very big credit limit."

The less I knew about the stolen card the better, so instead I asked, "How did you get here, drive?"

"No, we took the bus," Mildred said. "But it left without us." She smiled and asked, "Any hope of letting us ride back with you?"

I sucked in a breath in shock. "You want to ride with us?"

"Well, yes. Why not?"

"I thought you hated my guts?"

"Oh, but I do. Hal's too afraid to call and ask his son to pick us up and no way am I asking my sister, Elsie, to drive all the way here. You know how she can get."

I wouldn't call Elsie either. As it was, she thought herself to be the social icon of East Tawas. "The thing is that we don't have much room."

"Oh, Aggie. I'm sure they can squeeze into the back seat," El said.

I nodded as I handed my ticket to the valet, and soon they drove the wagon up. He waved and shouted, "I always wondered what an 8-track was!"

I handed him a tip and waited until Hal and Mildred had settled themselves atop the clothing in the back seat. An amused Eleanor climbed into the passenger's seat and asked, "All comfy back there?"

"Yikes, I might as well be going back home in a lumber wagon!" Mildred shrieked.

"I'm sure I can arrange that if you'd like," I taunted her.

Indicating my attire, she said, "Sweatpants do nothing for your figure, Agnes."

I gnashed my teeth together and delighted in taking off in a roar, making a hard turn fast enough to watch Mildred topple over in the back seat.

Mildred righted herself and asked, "Are you nuts?"

"Maybe in the future you should just keep your yap shut!"

Mildred gasped. "Why you little—"

Eleanor gave Mildred a harsh look. "You better just shush dear before she leaves you two on the side of the road."

"Two of us?" Hal spat. "I haven't said a word." Pointing toward Mildred, he said, "It was all her."

"Thanks a lot, Hal. I thought we were in this together. Has Agnes gotten to you, too?"

"Keep quiet, woman. Agnes was decent enough to drive us home. The least you could do is be nicer to her."

"She slept with my husband."

"That happened so many years ago," Eleanor said. "Maybe it's about time you just forgot about it."

Mildred folded her arms over her chest. "Easy for you to say."

"I'll have you know my ex-husband stepped out on me too," Eleanor volunteered. "I just never blamed the floozies." El stopped talking when I groaned. "No offense, Agnes, but as I was saying, it was my husband's fault for doing what he did and he's the one who deserves all the blame."

Mildred puffed out her chest. "Fine, I'll drop it then, but I hope you don't expect me to become Agnes' friend because that just isn't going to happen."

"I agree with that one," I said. Mildred might drop this, but it was far from over. I just knew she'd never let it go gracefully.

I turned up the radio and soon both Mildred and Hal were snoring away.

Keeping my eyes peeled to the road I said, "So El. What do you think we can do to help Sheriff Peterson with the election?"

"Maybe we could try to keep our noses out of his investigations."

"Thank goodness there isn't one happening right now."

***

A few hours later, I drove up US 23 and turned left on Newman Street. Just past the business district stood a yellow two-story, a once impressive Victorian home. I stared at the peeling painted exterior in disgust. It was awful to see the once pristine home in such a state of disrepair. I pulled up to the curb and asked Hal in total disbelief, "You're staying here?"

"Yup, my damn son didn't want me living with him. Can you imagine that?"

Remembering Hal peeing into a trash, I can't say I blame ole Peterson. I simply smiled instead. "Isn't this house used for rentals?"

"Yes, and they are a big pain in the ass. Always bothering me with their loud music and such. I stay on the bottom floor with Raul. Luckily I have a shitter downstairs so I don't have to climb those infernal stairs."

I was too curious to stay put, so El and I followed Hal and Mildred to the door. As the door swung open, we gasped in unison. A man was crumpled at the foot of the stairs, his head in a puddle of dark blood! Mildred screamed at the top of her lungs while El gripped my arm, digging her nails into me.

I knelt to check his pulse and shuddered as blood saturated the knees of my pink sweatpants. "No pulse," I announced. "Call 911, El."

I stared into Hal's bulging brown eyes and asked, "Was he here when you left town, Hal?"

"Of course not." He went on to say, "He probably accidentally toppled down the stairs."

"With help?"

"Don't you dare look at me like that, Agnes Barton, or none of you! I'm a frail old man. How could I kill him?"

I shook my head. "I thought you said he fell down the stairs on accident?"

"Because I knew damn well what you were thinking. You have very accusing eyes."

El, still white faced, agreed, "I know, right? Are you ready for me to call in the law?"

"I already told you to do that." I rolled my eyes. Oh great. I can already hear this one on the news, or better yet from Sheriff Peterson. This *so* wasn't the time.

El's fat fingers punched in the buttons of her cell and told 911 that a body had been found and gave the address to the operator. She then hung up, ignoring the operator's request for more information.

Within minutes sirens blared, squad cars screeched to a halt up front, and feet pounded up the few steps that led to the door. Trooper Sales was in the door first, his eyes shifting to my blood stained sweatpants. Next came a wide-eyed Sheriff Peterson. He took in the scene, focusing on his father, Hal, who at this point had his head down.

Trooper Sales swallowed hard and asked, "Who found the body?"

"We all did," I volunteered. "We just got here and he was already dead."

"He had to have been dead awhile," El added.

"True, El," I said. "The blood has turned dark and it's brown where it landed on the carpet."

Trooper Sales cut in. "Time of death will be determined by the coroner. I appreciate your input, but I'd rather you butted out and just answer my questions."

"Yeah, you old folks are in a heap of trouble," Sheriff Peterson suggested. "So you all arrived at the same time?"

"Yes."

"Why were you and Eleanor even here? I know you're not friends with my father and you're certainly not friends with Mildred."

"You got that one right," Mildred blurted out. "She slept with my husband."

"That was years ago," El retorted. "You said you were gonna drop it."

Trooper Sales waved his hands. "Ladies, please. Does anyone know who the dead guy is?"

"It's Raul, my father's companion," Peterson announced. "Dad, when was the last time you saw him?"

"I'm not sure you should even be involved in this investigation, Peterson," I said. "I mean it could be interpreted as a conflict of interest since Hal is your father."

"You sound like you think my father is guilty of some crime here. This might all just be an accident. Plenty of people fall to their death down stairs."

I butted in and pointed out, "Is that the sheriff in you saying that, or the son in you? I highly doubt you'd jump to that conclusion if it was someone other than your father."

"Aggie's right. If it was us, you'd have us in the back of your squad car already," El said.

"I'm the sheriff in this town and there is no way I'm not investigating this. I was just trying to make sense of the situation."

"I agree with Agnes here," Trooper Sales said. "Maybe you should let the state police handle the investigation. You are in the midst of an election, you know."

"I don't care about that. I can be objective," Peterson reassured Sales.

"Fine then. We'll discuss this privately later."

"When was the last time any of you saw Raul alive?" Peterson asked.

We all looked at Hal as he admitted, "It was probably me, but there are tenants, you know."

"Which we will be checking out, but dad, when was the last time you saw Raul?"

Hal met his son's eyes and shuffled his feet nervously. "A few days ago. Before my road trip."

"I remember people were saying your father was missing. Remember, Peterson?"

"I just figured Raul took him on a trip. I hired that man to stay with my father at all times."

"Which he did, too," Hal said. "He wouldn't even let me use the shitter without making me leave the door open a crack. Have you ever tried to use the toilet with some hulking fella watching you the whole time? It's like I was back at the nursing home."

"It was for your own safety, dad. So did Raul know you left?"

"Of course not! He'd never allow that. Mildred and me snuck out early in the morning. That's when the bus leaves, early."

"So Mildred was here too?" I blurted out.

Mildred's hand flew to her hips. "And that means what? I pushed him down the stairs, Agnes?"

"I don't recall anyone saying that, Mildred. Guilty conscience, perhaps."

Trooper Sales wrote in his little notebook and cut in before Mildred had a chance to retort. "I'd like Hal's and Mildred's social security numbers."

"What in the hell for?" Hal shouted. "Like I'd trust you with my personal information. The last thing I need is for you to steal my identity."

"Its standard procedure, dad."

Hal pulled out his wallet and a credit card flopped to the floor. Sales picked it up and stared at the Visa card, then stoically asked, "What are you doing with Raul Perez's credit card?"

I bit my lip, not wanting to pipe in.

"Well, I-I," Hal began. "It's kinda complicated."

"He told us that Raul gave it to Hal for safekeeping," El spit out. "Don't look at me like that, Aggie. It's better to just tell them because they're gonna find out and that will make us all look guilty."

Yeah, like she just hadn't implicated us in fraud. "He did tell us that, but I insisted that he stop using the card," I told Sales.

"Oh, so he was actually using the card then?"

"We never saw him using it. He told us he was using it," El added.

Sales looked straight at El and grilled her, his ink pen poised on his notebook. "And where was he using it at?"

"At Soaring Eagle Casino in Mt. Pleasant," El admitted.

Hal slapped a hand over her head. "Oh great. Why not shoot me right now. You know they're gonna arrest me now, El!"

"It's not my fault you stole the credit card. Who put you up to that… Mildred?"

"I most certainly did not!" Mildred shouted.

"But you knew he was using the card, Mildred," I pointed out.

"Well… "

"You're his accomplice, even if it was after the fact," I added.

"I didn't even know anything about the credit card until later. Hal promised me he'd pay Raul back when he won."

"Highly unlikely. I should have just called the cops when I found out," I said.

"So why didn't you?" Sales asked.

"Because he took off. I planned to drag him back to East Tawas whether he wanted to or not."

"They have an expression for that," Hal spat. "False imprisonment."

"I just didn't want to see you get into any more trouble."

"Looks like we're all in trouble now, Agnes. Good going."

Trooper Sales massaged his temples. "Okay. So you last saw Raul two days ago, Hal?"

"That's the story and I'm sticking to it," he said with a bob of his head.

"Is it the truth or not?"

"Yes."

"There should be a record if Hal and Mildred took a bus to Soaring Eagle," I suggested.

"I'll be checking that out. So Agnes, have you ever been to this house before?" Sales asked.

"No. I only caught up with Hal in Mt. Pleasant. Is Hal going to be arrested?"

"We need to wait for an autopsy before we determine if Raul's death was an accident, but it won't help Hal that he had Raul's credit card on his person."

"And about the credit card?"

"If he used it, he'll be arrested for credit card fraud, but I'll wait until the reports are filed and I can check with the credit card company."

"Until then, where is Hal planning to stay?" I asked. "I can't see him staying here."

Sheriff Peterson swallowed hard. "I suppose he'll have to stay with me, then."

Hal raised a brow. "Really, son?"

"Mildred, you better ask your sister if you can stay with her for a while," I suggested.

She groaned, pulled out her cell and called Elsie, simply asking her to pick her up.

"Are you done questioning us?" I asked.

"Yes, I already have your and El's information from before, so you're free to leave," Sales said. "But one last question. How did you get that blood on your clothes?"

"I knelt in the blood when I checked his pulse," I said.

"I thought as much. Go ahead then."

"I don't suppose you'd allow us to tag along when you question the tenants?" I suggested.

"Agnes, please butt out. It's getting so tiresome reminding you,"

Sales said.

"I know, I know. You're so by-the-book that it makes me sick."

With one last look at Raul's bent body, El and I left.

Chapter Seven

Sunlight nearly blinded me as I made my way to the station wagon. I could grumble all day about Sales trying to stop us from investigating, but what's the point. Once we settled ourselves in the wagon, I said, "We'll just have to come back later to question the tenants."

"Hal sure looks guilty here. You don't think he'd do it, do you?"

"If you mean pushing Raul to his death, no. He might be a crotchety old man, but I just don't see him capable of murder. Maybe it was an accident."

"Raul was only in his thirties, though. Seems too young to die like that."

"I agree, El. I just hope Peterson removes himself from the case before it hurts him in the election."

"He almost has, too. I'm sure Trooper Sales will convince him. He's a straight shooter."

"I just hope the details of this case remain quiet for a while."

"You do realize that this East Tawas we're talking about here. I can't imagine any small town keeping a secret this big under wraps for long."

"True El, but I just can't believe there might be another murderer in our town. It's so unnerving."

"And I'm afraid it sure makes ole Hal look pretty guilty. He had the chance and a motive."

"I don't agree with that, El. Do you think his motive was to get rid of Raul so he didn't have to deal with him anymore?"

"Yes, why else?"

"It just doesn't make sense to me. Without Raul looking after him, Hal very well may be sent back to the nursing home."

"Then there is always the theft of the credit card," El added.

"It's believable to me that Hal just wanted to get away for a few days. Sure, in his befuddled mind he took the credit card and used it, but murder—I just don't buy into that."

"I'm not sure what really happened, Aggie, but let's be realistic here—no way was Raul's death an accident."

"I agree with you there. I just hope we can come up with another suspect. I almost feel bad for Hal in a strange kind of way. He's just so—"

"Creepy... disgusting... "

"Oh, El. Be nice. He's just lonely, and it's not his fault entirely that he does strange things. Us older folks don't always think rationally."

"I always do," El said with a wink.

"Oh really? Like when you met Mr. Wilson."

"Best decision of my life. Not that you have room to talk."

"Where is Wilson these days?"

"He went to Saginaw to visit his granddaughter. How about your sweetie, Andrew Hart? Where is he hiding?"

"He took his sister to New York. It looks like we'll have to solve this case ourselves."

"Just like we always do," El said with a chuckle.

"How about some ice cream at Fuzzy's?" I asked El, who nodded in agreement. I made my way onto US 23 and drove toward Tadium. I pulled into Fuzzy's and El and I ambled inside. We waved at Dorothy and Frank Alton, who were engaged in an argument.

"Frank, I just don't like the idea of Sheriff Peterson serving another term as sheriff."

"Why do you even care?" Frank muttered. "It's not like there is a crime wave happening in Iosco County. I personally think he has done a standup job as sheriff."

Dorothy eyed me and whispered something to Frank that I couldn't hear, but before I could even wonder, El was prancing her way over to the couple. "What was that, Dorothy?"

"What on earth are you talking about?" Dorothy asked with a roll of her eyes, smoothing a loose strand of her grey hair.

"It's not our fault we keep finding dead people," El volunteered.

I held my breath—Sally Alton stopped scooping ice cream—and all eyes were on us.

Dorothy gripped her chest, rumpling the gauzy fabric of her blouse. "What dead body is that? Who did you find dead now?"

"El—"

"They might as well know." El took in a rattled breath and then spilled the beans. "We found Raul Perez dead today. Dead at the bottom of the stairs in the old Victorian he was staying at."

Dorothy leaned back in her chair, dabbed her napkin into a glass of water and then pressed it to her forehead. "Th—That's just awful. How on earth did that happen?"

El pursed her lips and blurted out, "I don't know for sure, but Hal Peterson is looking like a suspect."

Dorothy leaned forward, but before she could say another word, Sally ran over to the table. "How awful for you, dear," she said to El. "Isn't Hal kind of... you know—old." All eyes shot invisible daggers at Sally and she swallowed hard. "Sorry."

"Eleanor," I chastised her. "We were planning to keep Raul's death under wraps, remember?"

"I know, but Dorothy was saying—"

"I never heard her say a word, and how did you when she whispered to Frank?"

"I heard her loud and clear. Wherever Agnes and Eleanor go, there is sure to be a dead body discovered soon."

I glared at Dorothy. "Did you say that?"

"Well, it's kinda true. You girls are always in the thick of it."

"It's not like we plan it that way. It just happens." I frowned. "I don't suppose you can all keep this to yourselves? The truth is that we won't know for some time if this was an accident. I think it's presumptuous of us to jump to any conclusions or name a suspect just yet."

"This will be a nail in Sheriff Peterson's election bid," Frank blurted out. "Who is gonna elect him if his own father is involved with Raul's death?"

"I hope that's not the case. Hal Peterson used to be a sheriff himself and it's doubtful that he would intentionally harm anyone."

"Obviously you haven't seen the old man in action," Dorothy said. "Word is that he has dementia. What if he killed Raul and simply forgot all about it?"

"I see. Well, we all have had our moments. I'm going to wait to hear the coroner's report before making any further comment." I elbowed El in her ribs. "I thought we came here to have some ice cream."

El nodded and we made our way to the counter, watching in delight as Sally made our orders; pineapple sundae for me, and banana split for El. Life was good. We wandered to our table and I tuned out Dorothy and Frank. "Next time lets be in agreement, El."

With raised spoon she spit out. "About what?"

"Trooper Sales already frowns on us poking our noses in his investigations. The least we can do is keep privy information to ourselves. It might hurt their investigation."

"I see. I'm sorry. I'm just so bad at keeping my mouth shut sometimes." She spooned in more ice cream and asked, "So what's next?"

"We might as well get your Cadillac out of impound before they tack on more of a fee."

"I mean investigations-wise."

"We'll question the tenants tomorrow."

We finished our ice cream and I waited for El to return from the bathroom. Dorothy and Frank Alton had left, but there was a man seated near the door that I hadn't noticed earlier. Who was he and why was he staring me down? Instead of waiting around, I walked over to him. I extended my hand and introduced myself. "I'm Agnes Barton. Are you new in town?"

"Just passing through. I had no idea East Tawas was so noteworthy."

"Sure is. It's a great tourist town."

He took a drink of his water and continued, "I overheard what you were saying earlier, about the death of Raul Perez. I had no idea he died."

"Do you know him?"

"We were acquaintances. I had hoped to look him up, but I see that won't be possible now."

My lips formed a line. "Not friends?"

"Nope."

"Were you in business together?"

"My but you're inquisitive. I'd rather not say."

"Did you by chance stop by and see him a few days ago, possibly help him down the stairs?"

"You think I killed him, then?"

"I never said you killed him, but you do admit you knew him and he is, well... dead. Quite a coincidence, don't you think?"

"It's a coincidence just because I was acquainted with the man?"

"Stranger things have happened."

"Is that your educated guess, or is it because I'm unknown to you? A stranger in town."

"I can't say, yet, but I'm curious about you, like what your name is."

"If you're half the investigator you claim to be, Mrs. Barton, I'm sure you'll figure it out."

El returned and stood next to me as I watched the tall thin man get into a black sedan and tear out of the drive.

"What gives, Aggie?"

"That man just told me he was an acquaintance of Raul Perez, but he wouldn't give me his name. He sure knew my name though."

"That's strange. He could be a person of interest," El agreed. "There might be more to this case than what meets the eye. Raul is from Mexico, right? Maybe that's where they knew each other."

"Yes, but Raul has to be legal and this man didn't look Hispanic to me. He looked like a goon."

El shuddered. "I hope we're not back to goons with guns. We might have to check out Raul's legal status."

"I wonder who we could ask about that?"

"Sheriff Peterson might be inclined to tell you. I mean, if it might help get his father off the hot seat."

I shook my head. "No way will that man ever volunteer that kind of information to *me* of all people."

We left and drove to the impound yard, where I raised a brow at the fee. "Two hundred dollars?" I asked the overweight man who was stuffed into his garage monkey suit.

"Wait until tomorrow and it will be more."

"Fine," I growled, slapping down the money. We then were directed into a junkyard where the Cadillac was parked alongside a tractor. "Seriously, they impounded a tractor? This just isn't right. Why didn't they just leave our car at the beach parking lot? It's not like we were in jail all that long."

"How is the County gonna get extra money then?" El laughed.

El cranked up the engine and took out a sign on the way out of the lot as she swerved back onto US 23, heading for home. I had all but forgotten about Mr. Tinkles until I got back to my camper. He had wound his chain around the picnic table and only had two inches to spare. Any less than that and the poor dog would have hung himself. I could just see that. However would I explain that to Eleanor or to my fellow campers? Now, while I didn't care much for dogs, I didn't want to see one harmed either, at least not at my campsite.

I untangled the dog and led him into the trailer where he toddled to Duchesses' water dish and lapped it all up. Duchess stretched once and curled back up into a ball, ignoring both Mr. Tinkles and me.

The door flung open and Martha appeared wearing only a pink string bikini and a smile. "It's about time you came back home. I had worried my station wagon had left you stranded somewhere."

"Nope, but El and I had a little adventure." It was then that I told Martha about what happened at Soaring Eagle and how we discovered Raul's body.

"Wow, mom. How awful. Raul seemed like such a nice guy."

I smiled. "Did you know him personally?"

"Geez, Mom. I don't hook up with everyone in town, you know."

"I don't remember suggesting you had. I only asked if—"

"I've seen him around is all. I saw him at G's Pizzeria. That old man Peterson was sure giving him a time."

"How?"

"He was mad because Raul wouldn't give him time to be alone with his sweetie."

"Mildred?"

"I suppose, but she wasn't with them."

"That's not too much out of the ordinary."

"Hal is strong though. He knocked over the table."

"It was that heated?"

"Hal made quite the scene when they left. Raul had to practically manhandle him. It was shocking to most of the patrons, but you old folks can get mighty feisty at times."

"Do you think Raul was out of line when he tried to control Hal?"

Trouble in Tawas

"Raul didn't try to hurt the old man, just herd him out the door."

"I see. This kind of behavior won't help Hal's case."

"So you have a case?"

Before I could answer there was a hard rap at the door. The metal door tinged as it vibrated on its hinges. I opened the door to a stone-faced Sheriff Peterson. He wasn't dressed in his usual brown sheriff's uniform—he wore jeans and an American flag tee.

"Can I help you, Peterson?" I asked nervously.

He smiled briefly, and then said, "I'm sorry to bother you Agnes, but I was hoping we could talk."

Talk? Sure didn't seem like I was in trouble so I relaxed. "Sure, come inside."

He climbed the steps that led inside and stared into Martha's amused face. "Well, this certainly is a surprise. Can I get you anything?"

"A beer if you have one."

"I hope you're off duty tonight, sheriff," Martha said, as she retrieved the beer and handed it to Peterson who squeezed into a booth-like seat at the table. He snapped the top off the beer and the pungent aroma of hops filled the air.

I sat opposite him, ignoring the rumble in my tummy from the fragrance of the beer. I never drank the stuff, but Martha kept a steady supply in the fridge. "Is everything alright?"

He took a sip of beer and eyeballed me, then blurted out, "I want to hire you and El to investigate Raul's death."

"Oh? Was his death ruled a homicide?"

"Not yet, but speculation is centered around my father, Hal. It's just not plausible a man Raul's age would fall to his death down the stairs."

"True, but the coroner's report might not be conclusive. What I mean is, that even if the man was pushed, how would the police prove it?"

"It's the timing. I'm the Medical Examiner for Iosco County and I can tell you that Raul has been dead for a few days."

"So, about the same time that Hal claimed he left town."

He guzzled more beer and raising his voice, choked out, "Claimed? Hardly. My father may be many things, but a murderer isn't one of them."

"Maybe it was all an accident. Maybe your father didn't mean to throw Raul down the stairs."

"I grilled him on that and he would have told me if that happened, Agnes."

"If he even remembered, you mean."

"I don't see how he could possibly forget something like that."

"Heck, even I have memory issues. It happens."

Peterson folded his arms across his chest. "I just don't believe my father had anything to do with Raul's death."

"Are you still investigating this case?"

He swallowed hard. "No, I had to remove myself from the case. It's in the best interest of everyone involved."

"Who's investigating then?"

"The Michigan State Police. They brought the mobile crime unit to the scene."

"That sounds strange. I mean, why would they presume this was a crime at all?"

"My thinking is because my father is involved."

I interlaced my fingers in my lap and gave this careful thought, then said, "El and I would be happy to help you out. I'd like to clear Hal's name. Did you interview the other tenants?"

"No, Trooper Sales wouldn't let me."

"Sounds like a good place to start. We'll start tomorrow."

Peterson swiped at the sweat that appeared at his brow. "Thanks. I know we have had our differences, Agnes, but with you and El on the case I know you'll be able to sort this all out. I have faith in your investigative skills. I don't know any other person your age that can do what you two can."

"Probably a good thing," Martha interjected.

"Thanks a lot, Martha!"

"I aim to please," she said with a wink in Peterson's direction. "Another beer, Sheriff?"

"Please call me Clem—you too, Agnes. We've been through so much together that I consider you a good friend."

"Okay, that's it. You're cut off. I think the alcohol has gone straight to your brain."

He chuckled. "I know, right? What a shocker—us two sitting here at your table."

"I sure hope Raul's death is kept quiet longer," I said, full well knowing that wouldn't be the case, since Eleanor went to blabbing.

"It couldn't have happened at a worst time. How am I supposed to keep my cool when that Clay starts pointing an accusing finger at me?"

I squeezed Peterson's hand, which shocked us both from the look Clem shot me. "I have faith in you, Clem. For the record, I plan to vote for you in the election. That Clay guy won't do anyone in this town any good."

"He has a good record."

"Where? Redwater? I searched that place up on my computer. It's nothing but a small town in the thumb. They can't even have all that much crime there. You have experience. You brought down a human trafficking ring."

He raised a brow. "You mean you and El did that."

"Fiddlesticks. You brought in the water support."

"We worked together well even when we didn't," he laughed. "But that doesn't mean I'm going to make it easy for you. I still have to follow police procedure."

"That's what I like about you, Clem. I can always count on you being consistent."

"One more question before you leave. Raul was from Mexico, right?"

"Yes, and he became a citizen of the United States last year. I wouldn't have hired him otherwise." He stood and stretched. "I better get going. I don't want folks to talk. The less people know that I hired you the better." And with a nod he left, leaving a bemused Martha to shake her head.

Once he left, Martha said, "I guess you have an official case now."

"He never said anything about paying me though," I hinted.

"I had no idea you wanted to get paid. I thought you and El had fun investigating cases."

"It sure keeps us going," I agreed. "Did you find out anything about a Polly coming to town?"

"Polly?"

"Martha, would you get with it. The woman who might have followed Clay to town, the one he supposedly had an affair with?"

Martha took a sizable gulp of her beer. "Well, Polly and Clay were shacked up at Bambi's Motel, but the maid overheard Clay Barry tell her to leave town. He promised he'd send for her when the election was done, but I doubt that very much."

"Why is that?"

"Word is that he has an eye for the ladies."

"What is it about politics and women anyway? Even with an honorable candidate the women seem to flock to these guys."

"It's the excitement I suppose, and Clay is not only single, but handsome."

"Well, I hope that I don't have to worry about you dallying with the man, Martha."

"No worries there. I think he likes them on the young side. That Polly couldn't be more than twenty-one, the maid said."

"No sense in worrying about Clay right now, I have a case to concentrate on. If he cuts too much out of line, it will all be over for him. No way will the residents of East Tawas put up with any candidate who brings scandal to town."

I made my way for my bed, trying not to think about just how in the heck I was going to clear Hal's name.

Chapter Eight

I drove Martha's wagon into Eleanor's driveway. She was more than happy to switch cars for the day. I just hoped I'd return today with my Mustang still intact. Eleanor's Cadillac was partially in her garage, the remnants of her garage door sitting atop it. I could only imagine what might have happened.

I used my key and made my way through the house and found Eleanor chilling out on the deck, a glass of ice tea in her hand. "How did you get in?" she giggled. "I really should be careful who I hand my key out to."

"Eh, Eleanor? Did your garage door and your car have another disagreement?"

She shrugged. "Oh, you know how it is. I got the brakes and accelerator pedals mixed up."

Figures. Eleanor shouldn't be driving! "At least that will keep you outta trouble."

Her eyes danced. "Oh, do you really think so?"

"Probably not, but maybe you should leave the driving to me for the time being."

"Whatever you say, Mom," she taunted me.

No sense in firing back at her, so I changed the subject. "Eleanor, you're still in your pajamas."

She glanced down at her silky pajamas, like she had no idea that was what she wore. "So, are we going somewhere?"

"Yes, you knew we were planning to question the tenants at the house where Hal was staying. Plus, now we have a case."

Her eyes widened at that. "Really? Someone actually hired us?"

"Yes, but I'd rather not tell you who right now."

Hands flew to her hips. "And just why not?"

"Because you can't keep your yap closed, for one."

"All I did was share some information with our friends."

"Who, by the way, most likely spread the word by now. It will make it that much harder to clear Hal's good name."

"Maybe because he doesn't have a good name."

"You really need to be kinder toward Hal now. If you can't keep an open mind, how will we ever be able to convince anyone of his innocence?"

"Because he's not innocent of anything. He stole the dead guy's credit card," El reminded me.

"I know, but I'm not talking about that. I'm talking about finding out who may have wanted Raul dead, possibly enough to push him to his death."

"I'll be back in a jiffy," she said, excusing herself, and returned wearing a white suit complete with jacket.

"You're not wearing that, are you?"

"Yes, I want to look like a professional." She eyed my ensemble that consisted of khaki crop pants and matching button up blouse. "You need an apparel makeover. There are other colors to wear than khaki, you know."

"Of course I know. It just suits me is all."

"What you need is a nice dress and maybe some heels, show a little cleavage."

"What on earth for? I'm not trying to distract anyone."

"No wonder Andrew Hart left town without you."

"Andrew likes me just fine the way I am if you need to know."

"Sure he does, dear. How silly of me." She patted my hand like she pitied me.

"Go ahead and wear that suit, but you'll be roasting in minutes with that jacket on." I headed for the door, and announced, "Martha's station wagon doesn't have any air conditioning, you know."

"But... but," El muttered. She took one look at her Caddy and frowned with a full-on pout lip. "I suppose we don't have much of a choice since my car is incapacitated at the moment."

"I think disassembled is more the word, dear."

We left in the wagon minutes later, heading back toward East Tawas. Making the turn onto Newman Street took another ten minutes on account of the tourist traffic. I pulled to the curb and we walked toward the house.

"Oh phooey," El said.

Yellow police tape was strung across the front door. "Well, that's odd indeed. It's like they already believe Raul's death wasn't an accident."

"I'm sure it's Peterson's doing. He doesn't want us investigating."

"He's not on the case anymore, and he's the one who hired us."

Eleanor's mouth slacked open. "You don't say. No wonder you didn't want to tell me who hired us. Who on earth would ever believe ole Peterson would hire us to snoop around?"

"We need to keep this quiet. Nobody needs to know we were hired by anyone. Since we always investigate cases, it won't seem out of place at all."

Eleanor made a motion of zipping her lip and I hoped it was for real. "But how are we gonna get inside?" El asked.

"If there are tenants here, they must have another entrance. Maybe around back."

We ducked behind the Victorian where a staircase led to a door that was open. "I hope you don't expect me to climb those steps, Aggie. They're treacherous for old folks like us."

"Since when do you consider us *old*?"

"We'll just have to be extra careful."

Eleanor led the way and we climbed the twelve steps, squeezing through the door. Inside was a long, painted white hallway with four green doors. I knocked on the first door. A skinny man opened the door, glancing to the right and left as if to assure himself that we were the only ones here. "Can I help you old broads?"

I had to stop El from lambasting the guy. "We're here to ask you a few questions." When he just looked dumbfounded, I added, "About Raul Perez."

"I don't have anything to say." He tried to close the door, but I put my foot in the way.

I breathed in deeply when I detected a familiar scent. The fragrance was marijuana and chicken. I was sure of it. "If you don't let us in, I'll make a call to the state police. They might be interested in checking out the marijuana smell coming from your apartment."

His eyes widened slightly and he let us in, which led to his kitchen. Dirty dishes filled the sink and the trashcan had spilled onto the floor. I wrinkled my nose at the stench.

I pulled out a notebook and asked the tall lanky man with the messed up black hair his name.

"Why do you need my name?" he asked nervously. "You're too old to be cops."

I tried to act hip, and warned him, "I'd tread lightly on the old word, bro. It makes my partner crazy."

El gritted her teeth, but kept quiet.

"Alex Burns."

Perfect name for a burnout, I thought. "Alex, did you know Raul personally?"

His eyes widened. "Why you askin'?"

"I'm investigating Raul's little accident."

"Was it then? An accident I mean?"

"That's what we're trying to figure out. As you were saying... "

"He was a nice fella. He came up here to burn one with me a few times, but that's about it. He had to keep an eye on Old Man Peterson. He's the sheriff's dad, you know. I hope you don't plan to tell Sheriff Peterson about me and my pot plants."

Four pot plants were in the next room with warming lamps situated nearby. "Nope, but you might want to hide them better than that."

"Don't have to usually. I don't have many visitors."

"Wait a minute. Are you telling me the cops didn't come by asking you any questions about Raul?"

"If someone knocked on the door, I never heard it. I must have been in lala land."

Somehow I believe that is where he was most of the time. "They might still stop by. If I were you—"

He dodged over and carried the plants into another room. I helped him move the lights, too. I figured that way he'd be more inclined to talk to us.

We came back into the kitchen and he offered us a brownie, but I declined and wouldn't let Eleanor take one either. "Hey, I'm hungry," El pouted.

"I know all about those kind of brownies, and believe me you don't need one of those."

Alex tore into one, and after he swallowed hard, he said, "Suit yourself, but they sure give you one hell of a buzz."

"Back to Raul. Did he come to your apartment by himself, or with a friend?"

"He was alone."

"Anyone strange hanging around?" El asked. "Like outside."

"I don't pay much attention to that sort of thing, but you might want to ask the other tenants. Some of them are snoopy as hell, damn busybodies."

When we were back in the hallway, I said, "I sure hope we get more useful information from the other tenants."

"Alex is a brick short of a full load," Eleanor spat. "It's a good thing you told him about the 'old' thing. I was about to knock his teeth down his throat."

"I don't know why you get so sensitive. We are old."

"I know that. I just don't like *how* he said it."

I knocked on the door across the hall next. The door opened a crack and one green eye was visible.

"We're private investigators. We're here to ask you some questions about Raul."

A woman opened the door—at least I thought it was a woman. Her black hair was severely pulled back into a ponytail, revealing deep lines in her brow. Bulging biceps and triceps were displayed as she wore a green tank top that was tucked into her camouflage pants. Her feet were concealed in what looked to be army issue combat boots.

"Come inside, ladies."

We came in and two German Shepards stood at attention, barking. I hugged El tightly as I focused on their rows of sharp canine teeth!

"Shut your yaps," the woman commanded the dogs.

"Wh-What cute dogs. What are their names?" El asked.

She pointed to the black Shepard. "His name is Bite Your Junk Off and the other one is Fifi."

I swallowed hard. "How sweet. And your name is?"

"Trish Gunner reporting for duty."

I straightened and asked, "Military gal are you?"

"I was a ranger, and I'm anything but a gal. I'm a toned killing machine if my country calls."

"So you're still in the service, then?"

"Nope. I didn't pass the most recent psychological review. They discharged me, the bastards!"

It was then that I saw the weapons affixed to the walls of the living room. Rifles, handguns, and grenades! "I hope those grenades aren't live," I said.

"No. I'm not crazy you know."

No I didn't know. I really didn't. *Tread lightly, Agnes,* is all I could think. "We don't mean to bother you. We were just wondering if you knew Raul Perez. He fell down the stairs the other day."

"It's about time someone did the deed," she sneered.

"Why is that?"

"I don't much care for men, and don't like it when one bothers me."

"Bothering you how?" asked El.

"Trying to sweet talk me in the parking lot. Offering to carry my groceries to my apartment. Do you think I look like I need anyone's help?"

"N-No of course not, but men are just like that sometimes. It doesn't make him a bad guy, unless he did something else to you," I said.

"No. I only had contact with him a few times, and I told him to screw off both times."

"No reason to wish the man harm."

Trish glanced at the clock on the wall. "Is that all? I'm late for an appointment."

"Just one more question. Did the police come here and ask you any questions about Raul?"

"Yes, but I just told them I never met the man. It's not like I pushed the man to his death."

I bit my lip. "Thanks, Trish," I said, making way for the door.

It wasn't until the door closed that I breathed a sigh of relief. "That girl had me about shitting my pants," I told El.

"I know, me too. She didn't sound too sad to hear Raul was gone."

"She might just be a man hater."

"Or lesbian," El suggested.

"No reason to think that."

"Well, did you see her? I thought she was a man."

Trouble in Tawas

We wandered to the next door and I was almost worried what I might find behind door number three. El rapped this time around and a red faced stout man with a receding hairline answered the door. "It's about time you got here," he said, as he pulled us both inside.

"Oh, you were expecting us?" I asked.

"I saw another UFO last night. I can't live through another alien abduction, I tell you. What branch of the government do you work for?" he asked us.

"The Air Force," El said with a shrug.

I rolled my eyes and smiled. "Can we get your name, for the record?"

"Rob Glasier. I hope you can do something about those aliens. I don't want to be probed again!"

"I see. We were wondering though, about Raul Perez. He fell to his death down the stairs a few days ago," I informed him. "He lived downstairs."

Rob bit his nails. "Oh shit. They got him good. I tried to warn him."

"Have you seen anyone lurking about, possibly in the parking lot?"

"The aliens take human form all the time. They do that to trick us. Three nights ago Raul was arguing with an alien in human form, a tall one."

"How can you be sure he was an alien?" El asked curiously.

"Because his eyes were red. They can't change the color of their eyes, even in human form."

"If the aliens wanted to abduct him, how come he ended up at the bottom on the stairs?" I asked.

"They might have decided he wasn't a worthy specimen."

"What kind of spaceship did they arrive on?" El asked.

"It looked like a Hummer, but it could fly. I saw it hover over the garden before it took off like a rocket."

"Have you ever discussed aliens with Raul before?"

"Of course I did, but he wouldn't believe me." And without batting an eyelash, he added, "The other tenants think I'm nuts."

Not much of a stretch. I think he's nuts too.

"We'll monitor the situation, and don't worry, we won't let the aliens get you," El said.

Rob glanced at the clock, and exclaimed, "It's almost time for the UFO Files. Do you want to watch them with me?"

I walked to the door. "Thanks, but we are needed back at the base."

"I thought they closed the Air Force Base in Oscoda?"

"That's what everyone thinks," I said with a wink as we left.

When we were in the hallway I couldn't hold it back any longer. I leaned into El in a fit of laughter. "Can you believe that guy?"

"I-I know," El snickered. "Alien abduction my rump roast."

We stared at the last door, neither of us wanting to knock, but I finally did. It took a good deal of pounding before the door opened. An old lady with white hair answered the door, her sunken brown eyes looked up at me expectantly. Her mouth turned down into a frown. "You didn't have to pound my dang door down, dear," she said. "It just takes us old folks time to get to the door."

"I didn't mean to. We're here investigating the death of Raul Perez. He lives—"

"I'm perfectly aware of who Raul is and what he does for a living. It's no wonder he died like that. It was awful the way he ordered Hal around like that all the time. These walls are mighty thin you know."

"How long have you lived here?"

She counted on her fingers and then answered. "Twelve long months."

"How on earth do you manage those stairs?"

"Well, I don't. I have been here ever since that daughter of mine brought me here."

Oh how sad. That made me mad enough to spit nails. "How do you buy food?"

"I don't. Meals on Wheels brings me meals, and that lovely kid Alex next door runs errands for me."

"When you say you knew what Raul did for a living, you mean caring for Hal, right?"

"Among other things. He had a strange man visiting him, but he never came inside. They met in the parking lot. He drove one of those military vehicles. I can't remember what they call them."

"A Hummer?" I asked.

"That's it, dear. They're up to no good is all I know. What kind of men just sit chatting in a parking lot?"

"If you never left your room, how do you know what kind of vehicle he drove?"

She opened the door wider and led us inside, walking to a large window where you could see the parking lot clearly, with proper eyewear that is. Suddenly cats, like five of them of various colors and sizes, surrounded us. "Wow, you certainly like cats," I said. "I have one myself."

"They keep me company."

"I have a dog," Eleanor said. "A weenie dog."

"How sweet. Dogs are okay, but I've always been more of a cat person."

I cleared my throat and changed the subject. "Was Raul mean to Hal Peterson?"

She ran her fingers through her curls. "He did raise his voice at the old man. He deserves to be treated with some dignity."

"I see. Can you think about anything else Raul was doing that might be of interest?"

"No, but I'll be sure to call you if I can think of anything."

"And your name is?"

"Just call me Bessie," she said with a smile.

We left and I promised to come back for a visit sometime.

Once we were back in the car, I went off. "What kind of daughter would just leave her mother in some apartment where there are stairs like that? It makes me so angry!"

"I agree, Agnes. I wonder if we can help the old girl out."

"Like how?"

"I don't know. Report her daughter to the authorities."

"El, there isn't any law against abandoning your elderly mother or dumping her in a nursing home, but there should be."

"Besides Bessie, the rest of the tenants are plumb crazy in my opinion."

"And it seems like both the alien freak and Bessie saw a Hummer in the parking lot."

"At least both of them didn't see it hovering over the garden," El said with a smirk.

Chapter Nine

El and I piled back in the station wagon and drove back towards US 23. "Trish's comment about Raul is bothersome."

"Why would she say she wasn't the one who pushed him down the stairs. It makes me wonder if the opposite is true."

"I wonder if she was irritated enough by him to have done the deed. It just seems it should take more than that."

"True, Aggie. Maybe we should jot her name on the board."

"What board?"

"You should buy one of those dry erase boards so we can write suspects names and such. That's what they do on CSI."

"Great idea. I also picked up a laptop so we can do Internet searches."

"Wow, we're real investigators now."

***

Hours later we were back at El's with a magnetic white board we had affixed to the living room wall. I scribbled Raul's name at the top under the header, 'Victims'.

"Aggie, why on earth did you write victims?"

I raised a brow. "Since when have we ever been on a case where we only have one victim?"

"You're right. Forget I asked."

On the left side of the board I wrote 'Suspects' and next to that 'Possible Motives'.

"Add Hal's name first, Aggie."

"We're trying to clear his name, remember?"

"Yes, but until we do, he's still a suspect," El insisted.

I nodded and wrote Hal Peterson, and under motives I wrote: credit card fraud.

"So you think Hal wanted Raul dead so he could steal his credit card?" Eleanor asked.

"That's why I don't think Hal did it. Sure people might think he did it to cover up the theft of the credit card, but how long could you cover up the fact you used a dead man's card?"

"Too bad Trooper Sales found that card, otherwise they would be hard pressed to prove that one."

"I still think Hal's name would have come up. It's better to just let it be out in the open."

"I just hope we aren't implicated is all."

"We only just found out. I can't see a charge like that sticking." I paused, wanting to move this forward. "Let's finish up with Hal so we can move on. He was seen arguing with Raul, and some might argue that he wanted his freedom. That maybe if Raul was out of the picture, Hal would be free to live his life the way he chose."

"I don't agree with you there, Aggie. Without Raul, Hal might be sent back to the nursing home."

"True, another good reason why Hal didn't do this."

"Plus, how can they prove Hal did it?"

"Exactly, I'm sure they'll use a timeline, but it's circumstantial evidence if you ask me.

"Mildred was also there," El reminded me.

I added Mildred Winfree under Hal's name. I had mixed feelings about her. "She was there too, but I don't see any motive she might have." I put a question mark under motive for Mildred.

I next added Trish Gunner's name as a suspect. "She made an odd statement and she had a possible motive because Raul had bothered her in the past."

"So she says. I'm just not sure it's enough to want a man dead."

I added 'Alien' next.

Eleanor burst out laughing. "You can't be serious? You really think an alien did it?"

"No, but that's what Rob Glasier believed."

"He's also fruity as a fruit bat."

I added Rob Glasier's name with a big question mark under motive. "He lives there so I think he belongs on the board."

"I doubt he did it though," El said. "How about Alex, then? He knew him too and he lived there so—"

"He never made any weird statements about Raul."

"No, but how did he know about Raul if the police never spoke to him?"

"We told him, remember?"

"Yes, but still, put his name up."

I added Alex's name and under him I added Bessie, expecting El to interject.

"What did Bessie do?"

"She wasn't surprised Raul died that way for one. That's an odd statement. She also believed that he was mean to Hal, so that might be her motive."

"That frail woman. She barely walked to the door. You saw her, Aggie."

"Look, I know none of these people are viable suspects, but we have to start somewhere." I next wrote down, 'mystery man in Hummer'.

"Or alien," El laughed.

I next added the mystery man we saw at Fuzzy's. "I wonder if he was the same man in the Hummer?"

"But he drove a black sedan, remember?"

"True, but maybe he switched vehicles."

"You're fishing here, Aggie. We have no reason to believe that both men are one and the same."

I nodded and put another big question mark under the motive column. "I guess that's all we have."

"It's not much to go on," El said. "How on earth are we gonna find the man we met at Fuzzy's or the man in the Hummer? Maybe you should ask Sheriff Peterson if he could do a background check on our suspects."

"I can't ask him, and he can't do that. They watch things like that. He's not on the case and a deputy in Saginaw got into trouble for doing unauthorized checks that were not related to his job."

"Plus he's running for sheriff."

I stretched. "I'm hungry. How about lunch at Hidden Cove?"

"Sounds great!"

We left, and when we walked into Hidden Cove that Clay Barry was there with his God-awful mother. El and I squeezed through the round tables that were packed tighter than I remembered as we made for the mahogany bar. I glared at the leather swivel barstools. They were too high for either of us to sit in. It made my hip hurt just thinking about it!

I flagged manager Jimmy Baxter down, who looked more rattled than usual. He swiped his nearly all wet dark hair back. "Hello, Agnes and Eleanor," he greeted us. "What brings you ladies in today?"

"Lunch and a few questions."

"Of course. Let's chat at a table."

"Did you add more tables in here?"

"I sure did. What with the upcoming election it's been busier than usual."

We wandered to a table against the wall and I sighed as I slipped into the padded leather chair. This is the busiest pub near East Tawas. It was actually situated between Tawas and Tadium. "What I was wondering was, if you know if anyone in town was asking about Raul?"

"Not that I'm aware of."

"Any strangers in town that you can recall?"

"Are you kidding me? We have so many tourists coming and going in here that I can't keep track."

I knew it was a stupid question. "Have you noticed any Hummers driving through town?"

He scratched his head. "Sorry, no."

"Did you know Raul Perez?"

"Not personally. He came in here a few times with Hal Peterson, but I never met him. Of course everyone knows ole Hal. He's not the type you'd forget."

"Why is that?"

"He's so loud and spouting off about anything that comes to mind."

"He's definitely like that."

"How was he getting along with Raul?" Eleanor asked.

"They were arguing about Hal wanting to go to the casino, but I overheard Raul tell him it wasn't going to happen."

I leaned forward. "When was that?"

"Last week. Is it true Raul died?"

"Who told you that?"

"The police haven't officially released information yet, but they said on the news that they are investigating a local death, and Dorothy Alton let it slip when she was in here earlier. You can't keep anything a secret for long in a small town."

And how right he was. "Did they happen to say on the news if it was a homicide or not?"

"Suspicious death was how they put it."

"I see. I'd rather not say if it was Raul."

"It has to be, or you wouldn't be here asking question about him. I hope it wasn't a homicide. I hate the thought of another dead body showing up this week."

"What? Another dead body... this week?"

"Yes, earlier they found a body of a woman at the beach."

"Did she drown? Wash to shore?"

"I don't know. I just heard it is all. It wasn't on the news so—"

El and I scrambled up and headed for the door. We hopped into the wagon and off we went. We arrived at the beach minutes later and police tape was across the parking lot of the public beach. I parked and we made our way under the police tape, but we only took a few more steps before Trooper Sales stopped us.

"Where do you think you two are going?"

"I just heard they found a body at the beach earlier."

The trooper's lips curled into a frown. "You know I can't tell you anything."

I tried to look around him, but a yellow tarp was up. Obviously they were concealing the body or crime scene. "Then what's up with the tarp?"

"Go home, both of you."

"We're on a case and this might be related to Raul's death."

He stepped back. "I could only guess who'd hire you."

"S-She means we are doing our own investigation."

He shook his head. "Is Sheriff Peterson behind this?"

"Of course not! You know we don't get along."

His face stiffened. "I wonder, but I'm too busy here to worry. Either leave my crime scene, or I'll have you arrested. The decision is up to you."

"Arrested for what?"

"Interfering in an ongoing investigation for one."

I stepped back across the police tape. "Fine, but can you tell me if the victim here was murdered?"

"Is it a woman or man?" El asked.

He shook his head and walked away. "Well, I'll be. He wouldn't tell us anything."

"What did you expect, Aggie? That he'd let us see the body?"

"I wish we'd have found the body. Now all we'll get is a generic description from the news."

A news truck pulled up and reporters ran to the scene. Cameras were pointed at us and a reporter in a short skirt shoved a microphone in my face. "Did you find the body?"

"Nope, it wasn't us."

"Aren't you investigators Agnes Barton and Eleanor Mason?"

El smiled. "We sure are, and the police wouldn't tell us anything if that could be believed. I smell a cover up."

"We'll be looking into the matter is what my friend here means," I interjected.

"We found Raul Perez's body yesterday though."

"How did he die?"

I shushed up El. "We're not at liberty to say."

"He fell down the stairs," El volunteered. "We're investigating the case."

My eyes widened and I grabbed hold of El's hand and tugged her back to the car. Before I was able to get back in the wagon, I had to shove the microphone out of my face. "No comment!" I shouted. We sat in the car panting as the news crew surrounded us like hornets. "Good going, El. You need to learn to shut your yap. We'll be lucky if we aren't arrested later today."

"The public deserves the truth."

"Not when it puts our freedom in question. I'd rather investigate a little quieter. I can't believe you suggested there was a cover up."

"But Trooper Sales was—"

"Just doing his job. You heard the man. It's going to be hard to investigate if we're locked in the slammer."

El puffed up her chest and stared out the window. I honked the horn and fired up the engine. As I shifted the car into gear the news crew let us through. I made the turn onto US 23 and took a dirt road, driving into the country. When I saw a suspicious blue pickup truck parked alongside the road, I pulled over a few feet from it.

"What gives, Aggie?"

"I'm gonna check out this truck is what."

"What on earth for? I thought we were looking for a Hummer or a black sedan."

I rolled my eyes as I stepped out. "We have a possible murder at the beach," I whispered. "What if this truck was involved?"

"Oh, Aggie. If someone offed someone at the beach, they'd be long gone."

"What's it gonna hurt to check?"

"Oh I don't know. We could get offed ourselves comes to mind."

"Where's the adventurous part of you, El? You know, the one that isn't afraid of anyone or anything."

"She's in here, but she doesn't want to be part of checking out some creepy truck parked in the middle of nowhere."

I pursed my lips and then opened the door. "You can either come with me, or sit here like some kind of sniveling little girl. Maybe I should call Dorothy Alton. She was helpful on our last case."

That got El moving. She opened the door and pranced out, following me from a distance. *It's just an ordinary truck*, I thought, *nothing at all to worry about.* I looked in the bed of the blue truck and my eyes widened at what I saw—

Chapter Ten

"Of all the dirty tricks," I muttered. Inside the truck were signs—Sheriff Peterson's political yard signs! I knew they weren't being put up because the bottoms were covered in dirt. Someone had yanked them out. I was certain of it.

"Aggie, what's going on here?" El asked.

"Someone is trying to derail the sheriff's election bid."

She stared at the signs, and then said, "Maybe someone is putting them up."

"No, Peterson's campaign manager put them up a month ago. I remember distinctly him telling me that!"

"What do you think is happening then?"

Just then three women stumbled towards us—Mrs. Barry and the Canary sisters! My mouth gaped open... Mrs. Barry froze... and El moved into action. She snatched a political sign, and sure enough, it belonged to Sheriff Peterson. "What do you think you're doing here?" El blurted out.

"Yes," I agreed. "Obviously you don't think your son stands a snowballs chance in Hell of winning the election if you're stealing Sheriff Peterson's signs."

"Th-That's not true." Her eyes were focused on a nearby tree. "I j-just was—"

"Stealing signs," I interjected. "Put them back or I'm calling the police!"

"Why do you even care? Word around town is that you don't like Sheriff Peterson."

I made a stance with my nose high in the air. "That just isn't true. I happen to like the sheriff just fine. We try to let people think we don't get along is all. Your son isn't a worthy candidate."

Mrs. Barry was in my face now, ejecting spittle from her wide mouth. "That's not true. He's a well respected deputy in Redwater."

"Huh, that small town in the thumb? I bet the worst crime in that town is a dog on the beach."

"That happens to be an offense in Redwater."

"Are you kidding me?"

"No, I'm not. My son is more capable than the sitting sheriff. His own father is implicated in a murder."

"Whose murder?"

"His companion, Raul Perez. Word is that Hal shoved Raul down the stairs."

"From my knowledge, that was not released on the news."

"No, but Dorothy Alton told me. She was very helpful."

I'd give Eleanor one of my looks, but instead stared at the annoying Barry woman. "She's not privy to that kind of information. My bet is that she only told you Raul fell down the stairs."

"Still. If the sheriff's own father is involved, how can East Tawas count on him?"

"Sheriff Peterson isn't investigating the case, the state police are."

She waved a fist in my face. "He's unfit to run for office I tell you!"

I thought for a moment before I retorted, trying to gather my thoughts. "Maybe we should wait for the state police to release a statement before we start throwing accusations around."

"I bet you're knee deep in this. Ms. Agnes Barton private investigator," she taunted me.

I looked away, and then said, "Who told you I was an investigator?"

"My son knows all about you. Your husband was a Michigan State Trooper. You worked as an investigator for Attorney Andrew Hart and fancy yourself an investigator with your friend Eleanor Mason, who I might add has quite a reputation herself."

Eleanor rushed forward, arms flailing. "Let me at her!"

I held El back. "Don't give her the satisfaction. That's what she wants. She wants us to lose our cool."

I stared at the bird sisters, Mrs. Peacock and Mrs. Canary, who had their heads craned toward the trees, their eyes widening as none other than the Cat Lady appeared with a shotgun poised on the sisters. "You need help here, Agnes?"

"No, but maybe you should keep your gun on them until they return Sheriff Peterson's signs to where they took them," I suggested.

"I'm not doing any such thing!" Mrs. Barry shouted.

Cat Lady's fat finger was heavy on the trigger as she spat, "I don't care a whit what you have to say, infiltrator. I have plenty of room on my property to bury your bodies," she threatened with menacing intent.

Mrs. Barry threw her arms upward. "You're crazy!"

"That's kind of the point." I laughed. "Of course if you don't mind her cats gnawing at your carcasses—"

"She wouldn't dare," Mrs. Barry started. She then walked back to wherever she took the signs. "If you insist." The bird sisters followed suit, muttering out loud on how they knew it was a bad idea to begin with.

Cat Lady cackled, "Tourists," and then she disappeared into the woods, which I didn't mind so much. At least I wouldn't be subjected to another round of drinking her moonshine brew.

"That was close," I said.

"Nothing like a crazy Cat Lady to motivate Mrs. Barry into action."

"I had no idea we were that close to her place."

"Or else you'd never have drove down this road. She's not all that bad, except for her moonshine, that is." She laughed, but I didn't think it was a bit funny at all.

"I still don't understand how you can stomach her brew."

"Oh come on, Aggie. Believe me, I have had way worse."

I drove back into town, passing a group of motorcycle grandmas. They call themselves 'Wild Cats', which is about right. I parked in the parking lot in the business district and El and I walked into G's Pizzeria. A hostess led us to a lavender booth and promised us a server would be here soon. I stared at the newly redecorated interior of the restaurant. Sheer drape curtains covered the windows and a variety of Tiffany lamps of assorted colors hung above each table. The place was packed with locals I knew and tourists who tore into pizzas that were set on raised silver trays.

A server approached. She then pulled an ink pen from her khaki shorts. The purple tee she wore had the G's Pizzeria logo. She pulled a notepad from her black apron that was tied snugly around her waist.

"Hey, Agnes," the server greeted her.

"Patty," I acknowledged her. "I thought you moved to Detroit?"

She hesitated, and then said, "I did, but I guess I'm just too much of a small town girl."

El clasped her hands together, staring at Patty's round tummy. "Understandable, but I hope whoever has gotten you in the family way came back with you."

"Actually... Scott Wilson is the baby's daddy. We're getting married next week."

"Wilson as in related to Mr. Wilson?" I asked.

"Yes, he's not too happy about it either, but he's given us his blessing."

El swiped at her brow. "That's a relief. I thought I was gonna have to hunt the man down. It sure seems like there are plenty of menfolk these days shirking their responsibilities."

I bit my lip, saying a silent prayer. Surely El had sense enough not to divulge to Patty that my granddaughter Sophia was pregnant and that Trooper Sales was responsible. Not that Sophia was an innocent party. These days birth control wasn't just the responsibility of the man or woman, but both.

Patty spied a growing crowd gathering at the entranceway. "Can I get you gals anything to drink?"

We both ordered a Pepsi and away Patty went, returned with the drinks, promising to return to take our order after she took care of the waiting patrons.

Out of the blue, El asked, "Do you think Trooper Sales will marry Sophia?"

"I'm not sure she wants him to."

"You need to talk some sense into the man."

"I'm not so sure I should interfere."

The Wild Cats sat near us. They were all dressed in their motorcycle leathers. I nodded at the women. I kinda admired these ladies, freewheeling it down the highway on their Harley Davidsons. Lord knows with my hips, I'd never be able to do that.

Patty returned and took our order. Perfect timing to ask some pointed questions. "Did Raul Perez and Hal Peterson come in here much?"

"Oh.... well I... "

"Is there some reason you can't answer?"

"Yeah." El asked. "Did someone tell you not to talk about Raul Perez?"

"No, it's just that I heard Raul died, and that Old Man Peterson might have had something to do with it."

"Who told you that?"

"Dorothy Alton."

That made my blood boil. "Dorothy is just gossiping. It's not like she knows firsthand."

"I see. Well, Raul and Hal sure didn't get along very well. They argued frequently."

I pursed my lips, just as Eleanor asked, "Did you happen to overhear them?"

"Not exact words. I just know it got heated."

"Hal was upset because Raul kept such a close eye on him. Not a crime, since Raul was paid to look after Hal," I informed her, hoping to open the lines of communication.

Patty smiled. "You're right, Agnes, I wish I could say something nice about Hal, but he's was always so dreadful and demanding."

"And flirtatious," I added.

"He grabbed my ass a few times, too," Patty said with a grimace.

"Is that all?"

"I don't care much for being manhandled, and he's older than sin," she laughed. "I just can't imagine him ever being the sheriff in the county."

"He was though, you shouldn't take it so personally. Older men are just like that sometimes and you are a pretty girl."

Patty blushed. "Thanks, Agnes. I know you're right."

"Did Raul ever come in here with anyone else?"

Patty shuddered. "Yes," she whispered. "He came in with a tall man a few times. He gave me the creeps."

"I see. Did he do anything that would make you feel that way?"

"He stared at me like he could see right through me, if you know what I mean."

I understood perfectly. Younger women were easily startled by heated looks from men they didn't know. "Did you hear anything they were saying?"

"Overhear, she means," El clarified.

"No, they didn't even talk when anyone was within earshot. I thought that was strange."

"I agree. Anything else you could share about Raul?"

"No, it's too bad what happened to him. He always left such great tips, a twenty the last time I waited on him. I heard someone was found at the beach," Patty said. "Do you know who it was?"

"The state police wouldn't let me near the crime scene. We'll have to wait until they release the name."

"It's so unnerving. East Tawas is such a great town, but now with the death of two people, I'm just not so sure."

"Fiddlesticks," El spat. "Raul's death might just be ruled an accident."

"I hope so." Patty left and returned with our pizza twenty minutes later. I didn't ask her any more questions though.

We left and I drove to Trooper Sales' house, which was located in the country, nestled in the woods. The ranch style house had a wood pile against the side and a well manicured lawn. Trooper Sales' truck was parked in the drive and I made tracks for the door. I rapped quite hard and a surprised Sophia answered the door, looking quite green. "Hey, Grams." We stepped inside, where Trooper Sales was tipping back a coffee cup. I stared at him until he greeted me.

"Hello, Agnes."

"Don't hello me. Did you ID the body at the beach yet?"

He rolled his eyes. "You never quit. Butt out."

"I need to know if it was accidental or not."

"Me too, but until an autopsy is done—"

"I bet that is one busy coroner. Has Raul's autopsy been done yet?"

"This quick? Doubtful. Maybe you two should just cool it for a while. Aren't you supposed to be retired?"

"You should know better, Bill. Give me some details is all I ask."

"I can't. You know that."

"We're almost family here. I won't tell anyone you told me a thing."

Sales glanced toward Eleanor and then said, "Since when is anything kept quiet in this town?"

"It's not my fault and El can't help herself."

"Another reason not to tell you anything. It's bad enough already that I had to remove Peterson from Raul's case. I hope you're not investigating it."

"We questioned the other tenants."

He smiled. "And what did you figure out?"

I opened my mouth, but decided to clam up. "Why should I tell you anything?"

"I thought we were almost family," he winked.

"Maybe if you put a ring on Sophia's finger."

"Oh Gramms," Sophia said, suddenly darting off to the bathroom.

"Poor dear is so sick. I feel so bad for her," Bill said. "If only I had known I'd have—"

"Left your hands to yourself?" I answered for him. "Or possibly used some protection."

Bill's face reddened. "I wasn't planning for this to happen you know. For the record—"

Sophia surfaced from the bathroom, and shouted, "Don't you dare, Bill."

I fetched a washcloth and saturated it in cold water, pressing it to Sophia's brow. "Don't be getting yourself so upset." I sure wanted to know what Bill was going to say, but it wasn't my place to interfere.

She tried to smile, but it never reached her eyes. "I'm so sorry you're having such a bad time of it. I never had morning sickness," I confided. "But I know your mother did."

"That's what she told me." She sighed. "I keep hoping it will ease up."

"Just get some rest, dear. I'll visit when you're feeling better, but I really hope you both consider getting married."

"It's two thousand and thirteen, Gramms, not nineteen fifty."

"It was easier in those days."

"Huh," El said. "My husband still ran around even though we had a child. You can't force a man to marry you. It won't fix anything or encourage him to stay. Marriage is a two way street, both parties have to want it."

This whole conversation was making not only Sophia uncomfortable, but also Trooper Sales. "We're leaving. Take care, Sophia." I hugged her, and whispered in her ear, "I know you'll both do the right thing."

El and I left with a squeal of rubber on US 23.

"You need to leave those two kids alone," El said. "Let them work it out themselves."

"It's easy for you to say. Sophia is my granddaughter, not yours."

El sniveled. "What an awful thing to say. You know my son doesn't talk to me. I don't even know if I have grandchildren."

"I didn't mean anything by that, Eleanor. I'm sorry. I know you're right."

She brushed away her tears. "I guess you weren't able to convince Sales to give us any information. I wonder if anyone else could help us out, like Peterson."

"I doubt he'll tell us anything about the body at the beach, but I guess it wouldn't hurt."

I drove to the sheriff's department and we caught Peterson as he was walking to his car. His brows furrowed when he saw us. "Ladies, you have any news to share about my dad?"

"Not yet, but we have one or two suspects."

"Any cause of death yet?"

"Agnes, you know I'm off the case."

"But the coroner is your friend."

"If I ask him anything to do with that case, I'll be in deep trouble. I want to clear my dad, but I'm not willing to throw my whole career away."

"For all we know, Raul's death might be ruled an accident."

"I hope that's the case, but it won't help him with the fraud case the state police are putting together."

"Oh, did Sales say something about that?"

"Hal's days are numbered. He'll be arrested at some point."

"They'd arrest him?"

"It will happen. Dad broke the law and he knows better."

I agreed with that. He was a sheriff himself once. "He's not in his right mind though."

He smiled, rubbing his mustache. "I know, and believe me I'm doing everything in my power to talk Trooper Sales out of arresting him, but he has to. It's his job."

"I just can't see Hal in jail. I can't see that going well."

"They might just book him and perhaps release him on bail."

I nodded. "They could give him a tether."

"He's going to be even more of a handful then. It's bad enough already."

"So he's not behaving himself then?"

"You know my dad. He's ornery and asking me to lease him an apartment."

"He can't stay by himself."

"I know that, but convincing him of that is going to be tough. Perhaps I should have just left him at the County Medical Facility." I must have been glaring at him because he quickly added, "I know how that must sound."

"I understand. I hope you decide what's best for Hal."

"For now it's best if you can clear his name. Public opinion has gone against him and the coroner hasn't even released his report yet."

I took a pregnant pause, and then asked, "I heard the body of a woman was found at the beach. Any truth to it?"

Peterson licked his upper lip and shook his head. "You're really trying to put my head on platter here."

"I don't mean to. It's just that you never know if it might be related to Raul's case."

"You're fishing here."

"It's how I roll."

"Pretty hip talk for a seventy-two year old."

"It's not like we're a couple of old coots," Eleanor said. "Agnes even just bought a laptop and we have one of those white boards like you cops have."

His lips curved into a smile. "I see. You might want to check out social networking sites. It's a great way to check out the activities of suspects."

"Social networking sites?" I asked, totally clueless.

"Yes, Facebook and Twitter are the main ones. We also use them to check into the activities of suspects."

"Thanks, Peterson. And about the woman at the beach?"

Peterson glanced around, and then said, "It was a woman, but it might be a drowning."

"Was she a floater?"

"No, found her on the shore. You better keep that to yourself. I don't want to hear this in the gossip mill." He stared at Eleanor when he said it.

She gulped and nodded. "You don't have to worry about me."

"We still aren't sure who she is yet, but you'll have to wait for the news report. I've said too much already."

"Thanks."

"Who are your person's of interest, Agnes?"

"We don't have any names yet. I keep hoping Raul's death was an accident."

"Me too."

He glanced at his watch and I spoke up, "I guess we better get going. I'm sure there's somewhere you need to go."

"I promised the wife I'd come home for lunch. She's not too happy to be babysitting Hal."

We left and I headed down to the beach where hours earlier we weren't allowed. The news teams weren't there now, but the caution police tape was. I pulled up next to a white van and as I clamored out of the wagon, a laughing Martha whipped open the sliding door of the van. "You're busted," she giggled.

I peered inside the van where a smiling, youngish man sat inside. From the look in his eye, I knew Martha's day at the beach wasn't to get a suntan. "I'm not doing anything wrong," I insisted.

"Not yet you aren't, but if you are planning to go beyond the police tape—"

"Don't be silly with your suggestions. I'm sure the police are done investigating here or they'd still be here. I'm hoping they missed something."

"Not so sure about that. They were here for hours."

"Was the mobile crime lab here?"

"Yes. They left just as we pulled in."

I smiled at the young man. "Well, you two kids have your fun. We're going to work here."

"Carl, I'll see you later," Martha said.

As she made her way over to us, I blurted out, "We don't need any help. El and I got this."

"Oh phewie," she spat. "I want in on this."

"Do I have a choice here?"

Martha stood there, her white shorts gaped open where the zipper was. She zipped it up quick, pulled a cigarette from her cleavage, a lighter from her pocket.

"Since when do you smoke?"

"I always do after... you know."

I'd rather not know, so I let that one go. We yanked the police tape up and it snapped. I shrugged and made my way onto the beach. Hot sand packed into the sandals I wore, but I trudged onward. There was an area on the edge of the water that was marked out with flags with the number 'one' on them.

I gingerly worked between them and frowned, as fresh sand had blown over the entire area. I knelt and worked my fingers, sifting through the sand, but encountered nothing. Not a drivers license, nothing. "There's nothing here," I spat.

El helped me up, and then asked, "What did you expect?"

"I guess it would be too easy, but I was hoping a driver's license."

"That would be too easy. I'm sure the cops combed the area pretty well."

"Maybe." I took my sandals off and waded into the cold water. I then turned around, and said, "Is it possible that if she drowned, her body would wash to shore?"

"Not likely," El said. "There's no tide here in Lake Huron."

I searched the beach, which just days ago had been the site of a political fundraiser. "What if someone made it look like a drowning?"

"I like where you're going here, Aggie," El said. "Just like Raul's death looks like an accident."

"We need to find out if anyone knows who this woman is."

"Peterson said that we'd have to wait until—"

"How about a car? Maybe one was taken to impound."

"Like anyone's gonna tell us that," El muttered to herself. "It couldn't hurt to take a look around though, at the impound yard. Maybe we'll notice a new car there."

"But we'll need a distraction or some wild story. Maybe we could insist that something was left behind, like a wallet."

"Great idea, Aggie, but Martha could always flirt with the man at the yard."

Martha spouted out, "Hey, why me?"

I fixated on Martha's skimpy white blouse that revealed like *way* too much cleavage. Her daisy duke shorts revealed plenty of leg. "You're certainly dressed for the part."

She pushed her fingers through her wild blonde hair, and said, "Why not? It might even be fun. I'm always looking for a man."

Thinking about the overweight, greasy haired man at the impound yard, all I could do was smile. "Thanks, Martha. Team Barton is on the prowl."

Chapter Eleven

Martha rode in the back of her station wagon, allowing me to drive, which I was more than happy to do, since in my opinion, she drove like a maniac.

I drove up the beaten path and sure enough the same man was working. His wide frame wobbled to the fence as I honked at the gate. He opened it without further prompting, and strode to the driver's side door and asked, "You again? Did you get yourself arrested again?" He laughed with a snort.

I smiled when I saw Martha's eyes widen at the man.

"Thanks again, Mother," she said with a kick through the seat.

We all got out and I introduced him to Martha. This time I got his name—Ralph. "You see the thing is, Ralph, that I think I dropped my wallet out here when we picked up the Caddy. I was hoping we could take a look-see. I'd hate to have someone get hold of my personal information. Identity theft is on the rise, I hear."

He poised to move, and said, "I'd be happy to go out with you to look, but I'm sure it's not out there."

Martha moved into action. "Aww. I was hoping we could get better acquainted while those old birds went out there."

Ralph licked his lower lip, and with a smile that resembled a clowns face, he agreed. "Why not?"

I linked arms with El before he had a change of heart. We walked out to the middle of the yard where there was a blue Impala parked, and a few feet away, a rusted El Camino. "I'm opting for the El Camino," El said.

"Why is that?"

"Sorry, but I haven't seen one of those in years."

"I know. I thought only Martha drove an ancient rust bucket."

"Maybe whoever drives it knows Martha."

I walked to the Impala first and tried the door, but it was locked. I

87

tried to look through the windows, but they were tinted. I next walked to the rear of the car and jotted down the license plate number. I joined El at the El Camino, which was unlocked. "That's a relief," I said.

"The mechanism looks broken," El pointed out.

Soon we were rummaging through the glove box, but it was only filled with maps and coupons from fast food joints. There was a map of Michigan with East Tawas circled in red, but also a map of Arizona and Mexico. "If I didn't know better I'd have thought this car belongs to Raul."

"Why is that, Aggie?"

"There's a map of Mexico and he's from there originally."

El wrote down the vehicle identification number and license plate number. It was then that I felt over the ceiling of the car, and found a slit in the material. I pulled out a packet and shoved it into my purse before Ralph came up. The rest of the car was pretty clean. I glanced at the tires and noted how worn the tread was. Where had they found this car, really?

"We better get back to the car before Ralph becomes suspicious," El recommended.

I nodded in agreement and we rescued a relieved and frazzled Martha who was almost pinned to the chain link fence. I waved my wallet in the air. "Thanks, Ralph. I found my wallet."

He whirled with a snarl on his face. "You didn't have to be so quick about it."

"That's some El Camino back there. I can't say when I've seen one of those."

"I couldn't believe it when the state police brought it in. It still runs too, if you can believe that."

"Wow, really? Where did they find that at?"

He took in a sharp breath and smiled at Martha. "You know I can't tell you that, unless the lady here agrees to meet me for a drink later."

My eyes pled with Martha, and she swallowed hard and said, "Why not. Hidden Cove at six tonight."

He licked his lips. "Sounds great."

"You were about to tell us where the car came from?"

"The beach. I heard tell they found a body there."

"I'm sure it was just a drowning, not that it's any better, but we can't assume foul play is at hand whenever a body turns up."

"The crime lab doesn't show up if it was only a drowning though."

"No?"

"Not to my knowledge. I was told to make sure nobody went near that car, too."

I gulped at that. "Good advice. We'll be going now."

"See you later, baby," he told Martha.

Once we were back on the road. "No way am I showing up at Hidden Cove to have a drink with that disgusting man."

"Oh come on. Take one for the team."

"Very funny, Mother. It's about time you took one for the team, like found your own."

I wanted to try to reason with Martha, but who could blame her? Instead I suggested, "You could always just take your pepper spray. I'd hate to lose a potential witness. We might need him at a later date."

"Why are you trying to pimp me here? You saw him. He's so—"

"Your age," I finished for her. "You can't keep dating younger men forever."

"Let her be," Eleanor said with a giggle. "Let her have her fun. She'll be our age before she knows it."

Martha wrinkled her nose. "No way am I dating men my age unless they look like Johnny Depp."

"I was just kidding. I wouldn't want you to meet that vile man for drinks or anything else. Besides, I think he's married."

"Aren't they all?" El said. "He acts just like most of the married men I know."

"Did know, you mean. You've been off the market for a while, dear. At least since you began dating Mr. Wilson."

"How true you are. I just wish he wasn't gone now. It gets pretty lonely when you don't have any male companionship."

"Companionship?"

"Of course. Why else did you think I was dating him?"

I'd rather not say, but she was right. I missed Andrew too. I sure hoped he'd come back from New York. He was always good to have around when I needed legal advice, which might come in handy when Hal was arrested.

***

When we got back to the camper, I let Mr. Tinkles out and he shot off like a rocket—or as fast as a weenie dog could go.

"Oh great!" El whined. "You let him run away."

"I did no such thing. All I did was open the door. Maybe he'll find his way home."

El gasped. "I can't believe you. I told you he was an orphan."

"He's a dog, not a child, El."

Her bottom lip trembled and it broke my heart. "He was just like the child I lost. The one who lives God knows where, ignoring the fact he has a mother."

"There, there, El. I'll help you find him."

Leotyne wobbled over to El and handed her a tissue. "Don't worry. I can use my crystal ball to find your dog."

I opened my mouth to say something, but closed it again when the gypsy gave me a hard stare. El and I joined Leotyne in her trailer. Inside, the walls were covered with mauve, ornate rugs. Centered in the room was a table, and on the table, a huge murky globe atop a gold base. We each sat on a chair and Martha rushed inside, taking another. "I wouldn't miss this for the world," Martha muttered.

Leotyne dressed completely in black. The tattered edges of her dress touched the top of her pointy shoes. She raised her hands and motioned over the top of the globe like she was conjuring up a spirit! I wrinkled my nose at the stench of incense that she had burning on an opposite table.

Glitter inside the globe floated up and spiraled around, floating to the bottom slowly, and as it did, Leotyne spoke, "Magical globe. Where has the dog gone?"

It was all I could do to suppress a laugh at how ridiculous this all seemed.

Leotyne fixed her eyes on the globe and cackled in delight. "He's at the beach, but someone is trying to take him! You must hurry!"

El leapt up and ran out the door with Martha in hot pursuit, but Leotyne grabbed my arm with a bony hand, stopping me from following. "You must be careful. You're in danger."

I tugged my arm away. "By who?" I demanded.

"The man is coming for you."

My eyes widened in disbelief and I ran from the trailer in terror. On another case, Leotyne had insisted the devil was coming for me, and he was. I almost died in the attic of the Butler Mansion. Was this yet another ranting of a mad woman, or was she trying to warn me in her own way? I didn't have time to contemplate this right now. I had to catch up with El and Martha before either of them got into trouble. Had Mr. Tinkles really found his owners, or was someone really stealing him? While weenie dogs weren't a top breed, they sure were cute in their own stubby legged way.

I walked onto the beach and sure enough, none other than Mrs. Barry held Mr. Tinkles! "What is the meaning of this?" I asked Mrs. Barry.

"Give me back my dog, sign stealer!" Eleanor shouted.

"He belongs to a friend of mine and she's so upset he was lost."

"Bull!" El shouted. "I found him wandering on US 23 and he didn't have any identification."

"Give Eleanor back the dog. We're not about to let you take the dog without proof. For all we know you're stealing him for yourself."

"Hah," Barry said. "Poor Kimberly has been crying her eyes out over the loss of her dog."

"Kimberly?"

"Yes, Kimberly Steele. She works for Jeremy Preston back in Redwater and she's pregnant." Weenie ran off when she stopped at a roadside bathroom."

Since there wasn't a roadside bathroom anywhere close by it made me think this was a farfetched story, but Mr. Tinkles didn't seem to mind that Mrs. Barry held him. "I see. Is Miss Steele here?"

"No, but she's staying at Days Inn."

"I see. Well, hand the dog over and bring Miss Steele to my camper. Then we can sort this all out."

Mrs. Barry narrowed her eyes, but she set Mr. Tinkles down and El scooped him up. With her nose held high, El strode away. I gave Mrs. Barry instructions on how to find my Winnebago and left.

Once I was back at my camper, it was to find Mr. Tinkles on a chain and Eleanor sitting dejected at the picnic table. "Eleanor," I began. "Are you sure Mr. Tinkles didn't have a collar on with identification?"

After a lengthy pause, she admitted, "He had a collar on with the name, Weenie, and the owners name, but when I tried calling the number, it was disconnected. I didn't see no harm in claiming the dog." Tears trickled down her full cheeks. "I really love that dog."

"I know you do, El, and I'm so sorry, but this Kimberly person better show up or I'm not handing the dog over to anybody," I promised.

An hour later, an SUV pulled into the drive and the male driver ran to the passenger side and helped a very pregnant woman out. She had long blonde hair and was dressed all in pink, sky-high heels on her feet.

Mr. Tinkles yapped upon seeing her and I knew in that instant that the dog belonged to her. Eleanor loosed the chain and handed it to the woman. "Oh thank you so much," she gushed. "I had lost all hope that I'd ever see Weenie again."

I stared at the woman's blue eyes, and asked, "So you're Kimberly Steele?"

"Yes," she shook my hand. "Did you find my dog?"

I motioned to El, "No, my friend Eleanor Mason did."

El wiped at the tears that formed. "He's such a great dog. I tried to call the contact number, but it was disconnected."

"I just got married."

"In record time," I spouted. "Good to know a man steps up to his responsibilities."

Kimberly smiled, revealing straight, perfect teeth. "The baby isn't his," she admitted. "But we fell in love and got married."

"Oh, even better, a modern romance."

"This is my husband, Jeremy Preston. He's a lawyer."

I raised a brow. "I think Mrs. Barry told me you worked for him."

"I did before we married, but I got a modeling gig for a lotion line. You might have heard about it. Pretty and Pregnant."

"No, new one on me, but then again I don't shop for such products. My granddaughter is pregnant though. I should tell her about it."

"Oh really? How sweet. Jeremy, be a dear and fetch one of the starter sets for this kind woman's granddaughter," Kimberly instructed her husband.

He returned with a gift bag that was quite heavy and contained lotion and body wash in a quite pleasant vanilla scent. "Thanks for the free product."

"It's the least I can do since you two took such good care of my pooch. Eleanor, I don't know what else to say. I can see you're upset, but Weenie means so much to me. Maybe you could keep him until I leave town."

"I-I'd love that," El gushed, taking the chain back from Kimberly. "I promise this time to make sure he doesn't escape."

"Good idea. Weenie really likes to run off the chain, but you just can't trust him. One of the reasons he got away from me."

"I'd be happy to pay you for your trouble," Jeremy said.

"Not at all. It would be my pleasure," El said. "Do you know Mrs. Barry, then?"

"Yes, she's a bit rough on the edges, but quite nice when you get to know her," Kimberly said with a smile. "Her son is running for sheriff here."

My lips formed into a line. "I know, but we like the current sheriff just fine."

"I imagine you do, but Clay is a good man in his own way."

"Is he now? I heard word that he's having an affair."

"He's not even married."

Shucks, no luck with finding dirt on him. "Why isn't he running for office in Redwater?"

"I'm not sure, but not many people would vote for him there, not with Mrs. Barry's many lawsuits."

"She's filed a suit against just about everyone in Redwater," Jeremy added. "I sure don't mind the business, but I'm not much for frivolous lawsuits."

"Frivolous, you say?"

"Yes, neighbor complaints for the most part," Kimberly informed us.

We said our goodbyes and Kimberly and Jeremy left, leaving El and I to plot at the picnic table. "So, Clay is single and his mother is sue happy," I mused. "It sounds like he might be trouble for East Tawas."

"Or his mother might be," El added.

"I wonder if it's possible to dig some dirt up?"

"Maybe he's carousing here in East Tawas already?"

"Only one way to find out, but we have our hands full with this case."

"True, Aggie, and I'm about beat for the day. Maybe we should wait until tomorrow to plot further."

"Good idea." I ran El and Mr. Tinkles home. It was hard to refer to him as Weenie when Mr. Tinkles fit so much better, thinking back to when the blasted dog peed on me.

When I got home, I popped in a frozen dinner, ate and retired, hoping that maybe the coroner's report would come back tomorrow.

Chapter Twelve

Instead of waking up to the sun shining in my face, I woke up to the sound of rain pounding on the tin roof with a pling... pling... pling. I padded to the kitchen and brewed coffee, just as Martha stretched. "You sure read my mind," she said. "Although this is perfect sleeping weather."

I nodded and poured two cups of coffee when it was ready, pouring vanilla creamer in mine. We sat opposite each other at the table. As I slowly stirred my cup, I said, "I'm gonna have to go over to El's place today. I'm gonna take my laptop."

"You finally bought a computer?" Martha grinned. "It's about time."

"We were going to search on social media sites for information about Raul. I heard Facebook might be a good place to start."

"You'll have to set up a profile first. Do you have an email yet?"

I shook my head. "What's an email?"

"I'm gonna need another cup of coffee first, but I'll help you out."

Martha spent the next two hours helping me set up an email and Facebook account. Next on the list was Twitter, but my eyes widened when Martha told me I was allowed only 140 characters on Twitter. "140 characters? How dumb is that?" I watched in wonder as the feed moved so fast. "How would anyone read any of those posts when they move so fast?" I asked Martha.

"Who knows, but you can check out tweets from celebrities too."

I checked out Betty White's tweets, but all she tweeted was about her shows Off Their Rockers and Hot in Cleveland. "Why is everyone using the number sign?"

"It's called a hashtag and I'd be here all day trying to explain what it means, Mom."

Unimpressed, I packed up my laptop and took Martha's station wagon to Eleanor's house. I used my key when I found that the door was locked. Eleanor was in the kitchen cooking bacon. I breathed deeply as the aroma of bacon wafted toward me. "How did you know I was hungry?"

"Lucky guess." She eyed my computer bag. "What you got there, Aggie?"

"Oh it's nothing, just my computer. Martha helped me set up an email address, Twitter, and Facebook page. With any luck, Raul had accounts on social media sites."

"What about the packet you found in the car yesterday?"

"I forgot all about that." I searched in my purse and pulled the packet out. Unlike our last case, this one didn't contain cash, but a document. "It's a deed belonging to Raul Perez of a lakefront property with a beneficiary listed."

"Who's the beneficiary?"

"Maria Sanchez. I wonder if she's the woman found at the beach dead?"

"Who is this Maria exactly, I wonder?" El said as she piled my plate with bacon and then moved to fill her own. "A relative? Girlfriend?"

"Maybe we can find out on Twitter or Facebook. Peterson said that might be a good place to start." I pulled the laptop from the bag and opened it on the dining room table. Eleanor gave me the password to access her wireless Internet. Once I was online, I went to my email and checked to see if I had any mail. All I had was a welcome message from Google with a tutorial that I skimmed through. It also notified me that I had three friend requests. I logged in to Facebook, incorrectly keying in the password a few times, but I finally had it up. My eyes widened when I saw an unflattering picture of myself. Did I really look that old? My timeline was a picture of an East Tawas sunset. I'd really have to talk to Martha later about finding a better picture of me to post.

"Wow," El said. "This is so cool."

"Do kids say that anymore?"

"Not sure, but I do. This is so exciting. Go to the home page."

There wasn't much on there, since I had no friends. That was, until I accepted the friend requests. Within seconds I was able to see posts, one from Martha, who was one of the requests. Her post read, "Helped my elderly mom set up a Facebook. Consider this a warning!"

Eleanor giggled. "What did you expect?"

I also frowned at the ads that scrolled down, weight loss aids. How on earth did these people know I had packed on a few? And just what in the hell did LOL mean? Out of curiosity I typed in my granddaughter Sophia's name. Up came her page with a way too sexy photo of her. Why on earth would she post such a photo showing cleavage? There was also a post that read, "Gramms needs to come to reality. I'm not getting married just because I'm pregnant." Why on earth would Sophia post something so personal on a social networking site? Why, any kind of stranger or loon could read it. I swallowed hard and typed in 'Raul Perez'. His page came up with a picture that didn't look all that much like him, but it was taken at the house where he lived. His last post was three days ago, and it read, "I'm not a fool, and if you think I am, you're mistaken. I'm in control of the situation."

"What's that suppose to mean?" El asked. "It sounds like a coded message of sorts. Check to see if he's friends with Maria Sanchez. Check her info page."

I gave El a sharp look. "How on earth do you know this much about Facebook?"

"I'm not an old fuddy duddy like you, Aggie. I'm hip with the times." She giggled. "Actually, I went to the library with Elsie. Did you know she's on Facebook?"

I shook my head. "Why on earth would she be on there?"

"Knowing her, so she could be snoopy. Just watch what you post is all I'm saying."

Back to task, I went to Maria's page. Her profile picture consisted of a photo of her in a red string bikini on a beach that looked to be somewhere tropical. Her last post, "Things are getting weird here in Michigan. I'm outta here."

"She sounds rattled," El said. "I wonder if she posted that after Raul died?"

"It sure looks like it. We have two strange posts, both by people who might have been murdered."

"Look, Aggie. We don't know that yet, unless Peterson is willing to dish. Maybe since we have a name, he'd tell us if she was the one or not."

"Or he might have a reaction."

"True. He has to tell us something." I checked both Raul's and Maria's friend lists to see if any of them were friends of both Raul and Maria's. I found one that resembled the man we saw at Fuzzy's. "Harry Hunan," I said out loud. "Doesn't seem Hispanic to me."

"Who says he is?" El asked. "Just because Raul was from Mexico doesn't mean this man is."

"You're right, but if he's not, then what is the connection between the two of them?"

"I'm not sure, but with both Raul and Maria dead, if she's the woman at the beach that is, who takes possession of the property?"

"I'm not sure, but it sounds like a good place to start. We need to check out the property. Who knows, maybe the suspect is there right now," I suggested. I checked Harry's Facebook profile, but he hadn't posted in over a month. There was something eerie about his plastered-on smile full of sparkly teeth that bothered me.

I Googled how to do a screen shot and followed the directions, and did a screen shot of both Raul's and Maria's friends, just in case some of them decided to un-friend either of them. I was beginning to sound like an ole Facebook pro now. I could see how this was a useful tool.

I went to the board and added Maria's name to the victim list and Harry Hunan's name on the suspect list, with a double question mark under the heading 'motive'. "Not sure if this Harry has a motive or not."

"Or if that's even his real name," Eleanor added.

"I have to agree with you there." I called Sheriff Peterson and he agreed to meet me at the pier. Eleanor left Mr. Tinkles with Martha on the way, convincing her to watch the mutt. She happily agreed when she found out we had planned to be gone most of the day.

When we got to the pier, it was relatively vacant. It was sprinkling now, but not bad enough that I couldn't go through with the meeting. I greeted the sheriff. "Hello, Peterson."

He nodded, making sure that nobody was nearby. "What do you want?"

"Information. All you have to do is nod yes or no and we'll be gone."

"Sounds easy enough."

"Is Maria Sanchez the woman you found dead at the beach?"

Peterson stiffened, and after a few moments, he nodded. I moved to leave, and he asked, "How did you find her name?"

"Facebook," I said. "Thanks for giving me that tip, but I guess you could follow up the same tips."

"I could, if I was on the case that is, but the coroner came back with his report. According to him, Raul's death might have been accidental."

"Which means what exactly?"

"That there isn't proof enough to say that he was murdered."

"How did you find that out if you're not on the case?"

"He called me. Don't worry, I'm being very careful."

"I see. Do you want us to stop investigating then?"

"No, I still think you need to follow it through, unless you agree with the coroner."

"I don't," I said as I turned to leave. "But at least speculation about your father will stop."

"You should know better than that, Agnes. He's still going to have to answer for his theft of Raul's credit card."

"Has he been arrested yet?"

"No, but I'm expecting it to happen anytime."

Once we were back in the car El asked, "Why are we still on the case? Raul's death was an accident."

"All that means is that there wasn't any evidence to prove that Raul's death wasn't an accident. I think someone pushed him down the stairs."

"How on earth do you plan to prove that?"

"I'm not sure yet. I sure hope the coroner comes back with the report about Maria's cause of death."

"What if it comes back as a drowning?"

"We've had our backs up against a wall before, Eleanor." I reminded her.

"That's what I'm worried about. I just don't want to be on the hot seat again. All that this snooping in the past has done is put us in harm's way."

"Since when has that bothered you?"

"It doesn't, but I have a bad feeling that I can't shake. If Raul and Maria were murdered, that tells me one thing."

"Which is?"

"That the killer is good at murdering people and making it look like an accident."

"Don't worry, El. We'll be extra careful, but we need to find this Harry Hunan." I paused for a moment, and then added, "I'm not so sure where he is right now, but it wouldn't hurt checking out the house I found the deed for."

"Lead on, fearless leader."

"El, are you finally agreeing I'm in charge?"

"Not a chance," she giggled.

Chapter Thirteen

I followed the fork in the road and drove up Tawas Beach Road where, five hundred feet from the Tawas Point State Park, I found the address. I knew in an instant this was lake front property and I double-checked the address to be certain I was at the right place. Trees were tightly packed on either side of the gravel drive that turned paved as I cleared the line of maples and oaks. El emitted a sound between a sigh and gasp. "Surely this can't be the right place."

I gazed in wonder at the two-story mansion before us. The brick home sported a detached garage, and when we scrambled from the car, a gazebo situated near Lake Huron was also visible. "How on earth could Raul afford a place like this?"

Eleanor followed a stepping stone pathway that ran between the house and garage. "Or afford those boats."

Two red Baja speedboats were tied to the dock. I swallowed hard. "I just don't understand."

"Think, Aggie. A man in a Hummer was seen talking to Raul, and now it turns out he owns this mansion. Raul's also from Mexico so—"

"I hope you're not suggesting Raul was a drug trafficker."

"It adds up."

"No it doesn't. He was Hal's companion, and no man owning a mansion like this would be living in squalor."

"He would if he was on the down low."

I scratched my head. "Really, Eleanor? Where do you pick up all these slang words?"

"Dr. Phil," she said, batting her eyelashes.

"I'm just not so sure, but I suppose you are right. Where does that leave us?"

"We need to find Harry is what. He's the root of the mystery."

"I'm just not so certain. How many times before have we thought we had it figured out, just to find out we had the wrong suspect? Plus, we don't even know if Harry owns a Hummer."

El's eyes widened as she looked toward the house. I turned just in time to see a woman with flowing dark hair approach us—the material of her white blouse and slacks flapping in the wind. "Can I help you ladies?" she asked, looking down her pointed nose at us like we were an annoyance.

I pushed my shoulders back a notch, and said, "Yes, we're investigating a case and it led us here."

"Case? What kind of case?"

"A murder investigation actually."

Her eyes widened slightly. "Well, I don't know anything about any murder. They never said anything about a murder here in Tawas on the news."

"Maybe they haven't released any information yet."

She pulled a pack of cigarettes from her pocket, and shook one out. "They said a Raul Perez died at a rental house, but that foul play wasn't involved."

"I hope you don't mind if I light up. I don't smoke in the house."

"Actually I really wish you wouldn't. I have asthma," I lied. Truth was, I hated the smell of smoke and couldn't understand why anyone would do such a dreadful thing.

The smile on her face vanished. "Very well. I also heard a woman died at the beach, possible drowning, I suppose."

I went into full-on detective mode as I grilled her. "Why would you think that?"

"I-I don't know. It's an educated guess."

"Based on what?"

"What else could it be in a small town such as this?"

"Oh I don't know," El laughed. She hushed when I gave her one of my looks.

"Oh I don't know. I found a floater once and it wasn't a drowning."

Her green eyes widened into round orbs. "A what?"

"Don't you watch CSI? It's police jargon for when you find a body in the water."

"I don't watch shows like that," she laughed nervously. "I'm more into shows on the Food Network."

El rolled back on her heels. "Really? I had you pegged more for a Lifetime movie fan."

"Not at all," she insisted.

I smiled smugly. "We've solved a variety of cases right here in Tawas. In a more recent case a man was pushed to his death out a third floor window."

"The widow blamed a ghost if you can believe that," El added. "We're experienced investigators."

"You mean like Jessica Fletcher?"

"I thought you didn't watch crime shows?" I asked.

"No, but my mom was a big Murder, She Wrote fan."

"I see. We're just as smart and savvy as any television detective."

"Do you have any more questions before you vacate my property? I have a pot roast on."

Not appreciating her willingness to dismiss us, I asked, "Do you own this house?"

She pursed her lips, and answered with a snarl, "I don't see how it's any concern of yours?"

"It's just a simple question, but if you have something to hide—"

She folded her arms across her chest. "Of course not!"

"Well then?"

"My husband owns the house."

El smiled sweetly. "Just your husband and not you?"

She relaxed a bit at El's approach. "It's a tax shelter. He makes less than I do."

"Really? And what do you do for a living, might I ask?"

"I'm an author. I'd rather keep my name private if you don't mind."

Wow, how unexpected. "I love to read books. What kind do you write?"

Her eyes darted to the side. "I don't see what this matters."

"Just curious."

"R-Romance," she stuttered.

"Trashy ones?" asked El. "I love a good trashy novel."

"Okay fine. I write historical romance if you need to know, and none of them involve murder."

"Please give us your name."

"Sasha Murphy."

"You're S. S. Murphy the bestselling erotica author?" El asked, with stars in her eyes.

"Yes, but please be discreet. I came up here to write, not be bothered."

"I read your last book, 'Highland Honey'," El admitted. She motioned with her finger, touching it to her hip and made a sizzle sound. "Hot! I loved that book."

"What's your husband's name?" I asked.

"Harry, Harry Hunan."

"I see. And are you positive your husband owns this house and not someone else?"

"Yes, I'm sure. Is that all?"

"Yes. Is your husband home?"

"No, Harry won't be home anytime soon. He has business in Oscoda today."

"What does he do for a living?"

"I don't see what this has anything to do with your case, which by the way, you never told me what it is. Your case I mean."

"We can't tell you that, our client wishes us to not divulge any more information than necessary."

"I feel the same way. Harry's occupation isn't your business and I'm not about to tell you."

"You do know that this will lead us to believe you're hiding something."

She squared her shoulders and ordered us off the property. "Leave before I call the police."

"You don't have to get your bloomers in a bunch," I said. "We'll leave, but you might want to tell your husband that we'll be back to question him."

In a whirl she marched back into the house, and El and I hurried to the car as we heard the sound of dogs barking. "Hurry, Aggie. She's releasing the hounds on us."

We made it safely to the station wagon and I drove out the way I came. I made a stop at the state park and paid my fee, heading for the point. It had been years since I had seen the lighthouse at the point. It was the perfect out of the way spot for us to discuss our case.

I stared up at the still functional Victorian era lighthouse. As part of the guest keepers program you can stay at the restored lightkeeper's quarters and pay for the unique opportunity to be the lightkeeper.

"Why are we here?" El asked.

"Because I love it here. I'm trying to absorb what Sasha Murphy said. If that's really her name."

"You want me to check?" asked El, pulling out her smartphone.

"Good luck with finding service out here."

Soon El was frowning, and admitted, "How right you are. I guess we'll have to check when we get home."

"I'm not sure I'm buying a word that woman said. It's not like she was all that forthcoming, and how did she know a woman died at the beach?"

"Maybe you should change your approach. Soften your tone a bit."

"I was being the bad cop. You are suppose to reign me in when I go too far."

Eleanor giggled. "Oh really? I was under the impression you were the one who liked to do all the questioning."

"No, not really. We're a team here, El."

She doubled a fist and lightly tapped me. "We sure are. She did give us the name of her husband and it matched what we found on Facebook."

"I wonder what kind of car he drives."

"If he's the same man we saw at Fuzzy's, he drove a sedan."

"I was hoping for a Hummer."

"He might own one of those too, but what we need is reliable information. I wonder if one of the tenants saw more than they're admitting."

"Which one exactly? I hope you aren't planning to make me go back and try to question the alien man Rob again?"

"He'll be at Hidden Cove tonight. I heard he has a group that meets over there on Thursday nights."

I slapped a hand over my head. "Oh great!"

"Maybe we should bring Martha. It can't hurt."

It bothered me that Sasha knew a woman was found at the beach, but never said it was mentioned on the news. Who gave her, or how did she find out, that bit of information?

Chapter Fourteen

El and I brought KFC back to my Winnebago, and Martha grinned like a child receiving candy. "It's about time you brought food home. I was getting tired of hotdogs," she said, referring to the only thing in our refrigerator.

"I was kind of hoping you could come with us to Hidden Cove later. We could use some help," I suggested, with a wicked grin.

Martha's brow shot up. "Not with the guy at the impound yard I hope."

"No. Rob Glasier. He's one of the tenants that lives in an apartment in the same house where Raul died," I elaborated.

"On the news they identified the body found at the beach."

I gathered paper plates, and asked, "Really?"

"Maria Sanchez. They still aren't certain about her cause of death as of yet, except to say an autopsy was being done."

"That's to be expected. Hopefully they come back with something other than a drowning."

Martha scooped potatoes and gravy onto her plate. "Have you ever thought that's all it was, a drowning?"

"I'm keeping my mind open, but my gut says her death, and that of Raul, are related."

"That's what you always think. Everything in the world isn't related you know."

"I know that! Geeze, Martha! I'm not that one sided."

"Yes you are and as narrow minded as they come, which reminds me, by the way, Sophia called. You need to let her live her own life. She's not marrying Trooper Sales, you know. She doesn't want to."

"She wants to all right, but I just think under the circumstances, she's unsure of Bill's feelings."

"You know that man is crazy in love with Sophia. She just doesn't want to push him into marrying her since she's pregnant is all."

Trouble in Tawas

"In my day—"

"This isn't the dark ages, Mother. Leave those kids alone to handle their own affairs. It will all work out."

I shut my mouth and ate in silence. El shot me a sympathetic glance, but I knew there was some merit in what Martha had said. I can't push my way of thinking on Sophia. Maybe in time she'll come to her own conclusions, one that works out for both her and Bill.

Hours later, I changed into black slacks and a white blouse, whereas Martha wore skinny jeans and a leopard print clingy shirt, sky-high heels on her feet. Her hair was as wild as all go out, like something you'd see in the eighties, but I had learned at this point to keep my views of Martha's choice of clothing to myself.

We made sure to take Mr. Tinkles outside before we left. The last thing I needed was to come back to a trailer smelling of dog urine. I drove to El's house and quickly changed into black leggings and a floral print shirt overtop. She had sense enough to at least wear sensible footwear in the form of flats. She had picked out her gray hair to cover up all the thin spots, and I must admit, this is the most put together I have seen her since Mr. Wilson left town. I felt the same, too. Without my sweetie Andrew, I felt lost and struggled some days to even throw on makeup to look presentable. I had left vanity in the past. I'm in my seventies, after all.

When we arrived at Hidden Cove, the parking lot was packed. We walked in together and the first person I saw and heard was Mrs. Barry, loudly talking to patrons of the bar-slash-restaurant. "Yes, Sheriff Peterson is unfit to be re-elected as sheriff. His own father is suspected in a suspicious death and has since been arrested."

Her eyes widened when she spotted me. "And those women over there have been allowed to have free rein for far too long."

"That's Agnes Barton and Eleanor Mason," a thin-faced woman said. "They have helped solve crimes in East Tawas."

"That's exactly my point. They shouldn't be allowed to do that at all. That's what the sheriff and state police are for. All they are good for is getting in the way."

El had to hold me back, but then a male voice split the roar of chatter. "Now that's not fair. How would you know when you don't even live here, Mrs. Barry?"

"W-Well, I-I," her eyes round as saucers. "W-Who are you?"

A beaming Andrew Hart appeared from behind the crowd, dressed impeccably in brown trousers and white shirt, open at the neck. His salt and pepper hair was slicked back. "Agnes Barton is my girl, if you need to know," he winked.

My heart did a flip flop right then and there. Mrs. Barry and her crowd scattered and I hugged Andrew tightly to me. "I thought you'd never come back to town."

"Oh come now. I love you, old girl. I just heard Hal Peterson has been arrested. Is that true?"

"I know now. I sure hope you can help the old geezer out. He's not responsible for his actions," I informed him. I then caught him up to speed on what was going on and what El and I had been doing.

"First thing tomorrow I will. It's too late for us to do much about it tonight." He looked over at El and announced, "I heard Mr. Wilson will be home tomorrow."

El blushed. "Thanks for the info. I sure missed his tuna casserole. It's the best in town you know."

We all laughed, and Andrew said, "Oh, I remember. It's a specialty of his, but can he cook anything else?"

El looked away, and I for one was glad she didn't elaborate. I sashayed away from the glaring Mrs. Barry and we waited at the bar until we all had a drink in our hands, then wandered out onto the packed deck, but not enough that I couldn't see Rob Glasier's red face beneath the deck lights. He was currently leaning over the railing with binoculars pressed tightly to his face.

It didn't take that much imagination on my part to know what he was looking for. Why, it wasn't long ago that El and I had spotted a ghost ship, standing in the same spot.

El chuckled. "I bet he's looking for UFOs."

Andrew's brows furrowed. "Did I hear that right? As in Unidentified Flying Object?"

I nodded and crossed the deck to tap on Rob's shoulder. He whirled, nearly toppling a table full of drinks. "Oh, hello there. I didn't know the Air Force was planning to show tonight."

"Air Force?" Andrew asked. "Never mind, I'd rather not know," he quickly added when I gave him a sharp look.

Trouble in Tawas

"We heard you might be here," El started. "We're a little curious about your methods. Like how do you spot a UFO?"

"I have a map." He pulled it out and began pointing to different celestial points of interest. Some of these were stars, but he pointed to a spot above the Big Dipper. "This one may be a UFO, but I won't know unless it moves."

"It could be a planet," El pointed out.

I nodded in agreement. "She's right."

"There was a UFO crash last night."

"Really?" El tried hard to conceal her laughter. "Where about?"

"In Lake Huron. Why else would I be here?"

"I have no idea, but if it crashed into the lake, how come nobody caught it on camera?"

He yanked out photos from his vest pocket and handed them to me. Each of the pictures depicted a glowing light in lower positions, almost like it was moving. I wrinkled my brow. "For all we know, these are fakes. There is no such thing as a UFO."

"That's what they pay you to say, but I told you earlier I saw an alien at my apartment building. He's responsible for Raul's death. I saw him push Raul down the stairs."

"Saw him how?" El butted in. "Through the keyhole?"

"I had my door opened a crack."

"Why?" I pressed.

"I heard arguing coming from the hallway. When I glanced out, I heard a loud scuffling and then—bang, Raul tumbled down the stairs."

"You saw an alien push him?"

"That's right. He was the tall alien I told you about the other day."

"The same one who drove a flying Hummer?"

"Yes, but he didn't fly away that day. He drove away."

I rolled my eyes. "You certainly have your stories mixed up. I have a hard time believing the alien ever flew away in a Hummer."

"Yeah," El exclaimed. "Aliens have sense enough to bring a flying saucer."

"I saw him fly away I tell you, just not that day."

"What time did this happen?"

"It was late, about nine o'clock."

"Did you actually check and see Raul at the bottom of the stairs?"

"Are you crazy? I didn't want the alien coming after me."

"Did you call 911?"

"I can't. I was told if I ever called them again, they'd lock me up in a loony bin."

"An actual 911 operator said that?"

"No, but the sheriff did."

I shifted to my good hip. "I see. How many times did you call 911 recently?"

"At least four or five times a day until they warned me not to."

"And all the calls pertained to aliens or UFOs?"

"Yes."

It's no wonder they never took this man seriously. "Why didn't you tell us this the other day, if it happened?"

"I don't know. I guess I didn't think you'd believe me."

"Tall aliens with red glowing eyes is quite believable to me," I mocked Rob. "I imagine if you called and reported a man had fallen down the steps, an ambulance would have showed up."

"Yeah," El spat. "If rescue workers had gotten there in time, Raul stood a chance of living."

"We don't know that, El, but good point. You're just as responsible for not calling for help. You could have asked one of your neighbors to call."

Rob scratched his head. "I never thought about that."

"Do you know the neighbors?"

"Not by name, but that cat lady freaks me out."

"Bessie?"

"No, the one called Cat Lady. She doesn't live here, but she's always at Bessie's apartment."

"How would you know that for sure?"

"I've seen them in the hallway talking."

How on earth was that even possible? How on earth would Cat Lady manage the steps? El and I had barely been able to scale them. "I see. Is there anything else that you haven't told us?"

"No, but I'd be happy to call you the next time I see or hear something strange."

I pulled out a notepad and scribbled my cell number on it.

Andrew was expressionless and I wondered what he was thinking.

Had he regretted coming back to town?"

We walked back into the bar, where I saw Martha chatting it up with two men, one of whom was Ralph, the man who worked back at the impound yard. "Hello, mom," Martha slurred. In front of Martha were three empty shot glasses.

"Are you ready to go?" I asked in concern.

"I'm staying. Did you know that Ralph moonlights as a mortician's assistant? He transports bodies from the morgue to the Happy Bear Funeral Home."

"And you find that interesting?"

"I sure do. He actually travels around with dead people."

"And exactly how much have you had to drink tonight?"

She waved me away. "Go on home. I'll catch a ride."

"That's what I'm worried about, the catching something part."

"You're such a fuddy duddy."

"I am when it relates to my family. Since when do you date anyone your age? Don't you like them on the young side?"

She hung her head. "Mother, you're embarrassing me."

"Hey, Ralph? Does the coroner ever share information with you?"

"Sometimes, but I keep it to myself. I don't need that kind of grief."

"I see. So you don't know if the autopsy's been done on Marie Sanchez yet?"

"Who?"

"The body they found at the beach."

He pulled at his collar. "Maybe, but I can't tell you in here. Let's take a walk."

Martha's mouth gaped open. "Wh-What? I thought we were gonna have a few more before you took me home."

"My wife would kill me if I took you anywhere."

Martha inhaled sharply and followed us outside. We wandered back to the station wagon and Andrew cocked a brow, a quirk of a smile at the corner of his mouth. "Cute car. Is this like the Delorean?"

"The what?" I asked.

"You know the car from Back to the Future, the one that can time travel."

"Funny, for a lawyer who's sleeping on the couch."

"Actually, I'm staying at the Days Inn," he informed me.

What? Not staying with me? Instead of reacting to that one, I asked Ralph, "So what didn't you want to tell us inside?"

"The coroner said the woman drowned, but he's still waiting for a toxicology report."

"That's just great," I grumbled. "That's two deaths in town that are supposedly accidental."

"Sorry, but I better not get seen talking to you. I'd hate for it to get back to the sheriff or—" glancing toward Martha, he added, "my wife."

Andrew kissed me on the cheek and left, promising to pick me up when he went to help out Old Man Peterson in the morning. Martha swayed as I helped her into the car. "How on earth are you so drunk already?"

"I had three double shots, Mother."

I drove to Eleanor's and dropped her off, then back home. Mr. Tinkles was pawing at the door when we strolled inside and I let him outside on the chain. How I ever got stuck with the dog was beyond me. Somehow I just knew Eleanor would shirk her responsibilities.

Chapter Fifteen

Andrew stopped by promptly at eight, and I was ready and dressed in blue crop pants with matching tee. My hair looked a fright, but I managed to comb it into place. As Andrew walked in the door, Duchess stretched and rubbed against his legs. "Looks like she missed you too."

He smiled and set down a box of donuts from Tim Horton's and Martha and I were on them like flies on honey. I poured coffee and settled in next to Andrew at the table with a crazy looking Martha across from us. Her hair stood up like a rooster.

"So what's the plan?" I asked Andrew.

"Arraignment at ten."

"He's not on his father's case," I informed him.

"I bet not, but what does this have to do with you, Aggie?"

"The sheriff hired me to clear his father's name."

"I heard they caught him red handed with a credit card, though."

"He was a suspect in Raul's death, but it has since appeared to be an accident."

"I can't imagine Hal would kill his companion."

"Me either, but I just don't believe Raul's death was an accident. Hal left town about the same time that Raul died."

"Peterson really hired you?"

"Don't sound so shocked. He knows I'm a competent investigator."

"Still, this is the sheriff we're talking about here."

I stirred creamer into my cup. "I was shocked too, and I just don't know how to proceed with the case."

"If they ruled Raul's death an accident, then why are you on the case at all?"

"Because I don't believe it was an accident is why."

"If you keep this up, they might just decide to charge Hal with murder. Even circumstantial cases have resulted in convictions."

"They wouldn't do that. He left for the casino that day." I bit into a glazed donut then added, "He wasn't alone. Mildred Winfree was with him too. Why isn't she being looked at?"

"Maybe she is, but the simple fact is that most likely there isn't enough evidence to suggest Raul's death was intentional." He took a sip of his coffee. "So what do you know about the stolen charge card?"

"El and I tracked down Hal and Mildred at the casino. He told us about the card with some story about how he had planned to pay the money back *if* he won."

"Big 'if'."

"Yes, he lost big, but I'm not sure how big. El and I tried to get him to leave, but he ran off."

"And you couldn't catch the old coot?"

"The casino was so packed and he moved quicker than I expected."

"They always do when they're in escape mode. Where is the old man staying now?"

"At Sheriff Peterson's house."

"Wow, now that's impressive. I bet his wife is loving that one."

"I can't imagine Joy Peterson doing anything but running a charity drive of some sort."

"In East Tawas?"

"She's originally from the windy city. We were all shocked in town when he brought her home with him ten years ago. They married a few week later."

"Strange for a small town sheriff. How was he able to pay for that trip on his pay?"

"It doesn't cost that much to go to Chicago. Why would you even ask a question like that?"

Andrew fell silent and then shrugged. "I think I saw something about Peterson mishandling County funds, on a flier by Clay Barry."

I squared my shoulders. "All that Clay Barry and his mother has done is spread lies. I can't believe you'd think something like that was true."

Andrew raised his hands in a defensive mode. "Hold it right there. I was just asking, is all."

We finished our coffee and left in Andrew's Lexus LX, despite my instance that we take Martha's station wagon. I had gotten used to tooling around town in the relic. I drummed my fingers on the dash until we pulled into El's drive. Andrew's eyes widened when he spotted El's Caddy buried beneath her garage door. "I guess that's one way to keep El from behind the wheel," Andrew said. "But I think I'll call someone to take care of the door. We can't keep the old girl without a getaway car."

"I suppose not."

El strolled out the door, wearing a yellow sundress with matching sandals. I got out of the passenger's side and sat in the back, giving my seat to El who needed more room to stretch out. Andrew turned his head and gave El a peck on the cheek. "You look great, El."

"Thanks," she gushed. "Mr. Wilson called me this morning. He's back in town."

I smiled to myself. It seems both of us now had our men back in town. "That's great. More tuna casserole for dinner?"

"No, he's taking me out for dinner. I'm meeting his granddaughter, Millicent."

"Wow, that's some name for a young lady."

"She was named after Mr. Wilson's late wife."

"I'm impressed. I had no idea things between you and Wilson were going that great. When's the wedding?"

El snapped a tube of lipstick from her purse and pressed it to her lips, and then asked, "How about you and Andrew?"

Andrew coughed in response. "How about we change the subject."

I silently agreed, but remained silent. I had no idea why that bothered me. It wasn't like I had entertained the thought. I mean, I was quite happy with things the way they were between Andrew and I. "Are you nervous about meeting Wilson's granddaughter?"

"A little. I mean what if she doesn't like me and tells him that I'm not good enough for him?"

"First off. Who wouldn't love you, El? And second off. I doubt anyone would be able to tell Wilson anything. He seems like a man hell bent to live his life any way he chooses."

"You're right, Aggie. It's just hard when you have to deal with family. I don't know how to respond if he asks about mine."

"You don't need to go into detail."

"What if she asks about my son?"

I pursed my lips. "Just tell her he lives out of town and is too busy to visit."

"I have no idea if that's true or not. I don't even know where he lives or why he won't visit."

I felt bad for her and all I could do was empathize with her. "I know how you feel. Martha had stayed away for years, but she came back in her own time."

"Sure she did, with all her possessions packed in that wagon of hers."

I nodded as I remembered that day clearly, and how at the time I wasn't at all happy she had showed up. I couldn't blame her though. I could understand feeling lost after my husband had died and my children had gone off to college. "I still don't know where my son Stuart is."

"I'm sure he'll show up one day when he's ready. You have no idea where he is?"

"No, and believe me I have searched."

"Hey, Aggie. Why not look on Facebook?"

"Facebook," Andrew choked out.

"Yes, El and I have profiles on Facebook now. It's a perfect place to search for suspects."

"I see," he chuckled. "Have you turned up anyone besides aliens?"

"I know Rob seems like a crackpot, but he did see a Hummer and a tall thin man."

"Even crazy people have some merit," El added.

"If you say so, but personally I'd have to see that with my own two eyes before I believe Rob saw anything."

I would have elaborated more about our suspect, but Andrew had made the turn into the sheriff's department. He parked and we ambled out, making our way inside to where Sheriff Peterson awaited us. He simply nodded and led us inside to another room where there were chairs positioned in front of a desk. The judge wasn't currently in the room, allowing us time to talk. Hal was dressed all in orange, staring at the floor.

Andrew set his briefcase down and pulled out a stack of papers, then handed them to Peterson who looked them over. "I plan to ask the court to allow Hal home on electronic monitoring. He's in no condition to waste away in a jail cell," Andrew said.

"You're not telling me anything I don't know. He caused quite the ruckus last night. I had to come and babysit him all night."

"It wasn't my damn fault. How do you expect a man my age to pee in a damn urinal the size of a milk jug?"

"That doesn't mean you need to urinate on the floor," Peterson bellowed. "You're making me a laughing stock at the sheriff's department, and I might as well withdraw from the election because nobody will ever vote for me."

Hal crossed his arms and turned away from his son. "Send me back to the County Medical Facility then."

"Listen here now, Sheriff. I won't stand for you withdrawing from the election. Folks in town know that you're not to blame for your father's actions," I reassured him.

"Sending him back to the nursing home won't put you in a good light either," El added.

"I'm not doing that, but what if they send my father to prison?"

"Not likely," Andrew said. "I won't let that happen. I'm pushing for them to drop charges."

"Does he have dementia?" I asked.

"He does have some form, but he knows better than to take a man's credit card. He was a sheriff at one time."

I sure wish Hal wasn't in the room, as I was about to say something that just might hurt his feelings. "Nobody in their right mind would think that Hal is completely with it."

Hal sat upright with eyes bulging. "So you want me to act senile, is that it?"

"It works for me," I said with a curt bob of my head. "I know you were once a reasonable man."

"You got that one right, toots. Mildred was the one who suggested I take the charge card. She's quite convincing when she wants to be."

"Mildred, are you certain?"

"She said it was the only way we'd be able to have any fun. She's a wild one and boy does she know how to spend money."

"Mildred Winfree?" She sure acted like it was all Hal's idea. Maybe El and I had better have a long overdue chat with her.

"Are you prepared to tell the judge that?" Andrew asked. "I don't want you implicating her and then changing your tune when you're in front of the judge."

"Heck with her. She won't even pick up the phone when I call."

I gave Hal's shoulder a squeeze. "Did you call Elsie Bradford?"

He rolled his eyes. "You mean that bird with the loose lips? She told me her sister wasn't there and she didn't know where she was."

I wonder if that was all talk on Elsie's part. "I'll find out for you, Hal. I'm sure it's just all a misunderstanding."

The bailiff, Bernie, strode into the room, his keys clanging against each other. "The judge is about ready." He took his place near the far wall as the Honorable Mary Kroft entered. We were instructed to sit and she read off the charge; illegally obtaining a credit card for the purpose of theft. "How do you plead?"

"May I please approach the bench, your honor?" Andrew asked.

She gave him a hard stare, and replied, "You may, but be quick about it. I'm expected in Oscoda at noon."

Andrew approached the bench and they spoke in hushed tones. Andrew walked back with a hint of a smile at the corner of his mouth as the Judge said, "Hal Peterson, your lawyer has requested a psychological exam, which I'm granting, and I'm setting bail at five hundred dollars. You may enter your plea later. A stipulation is that you wear an electronic monitoring device."

"Oh great," Hal muttered.

"In the future, Hal Peterson, reserve your comments until you're out of court or I will send you back to lock up for contempt of court. Is that understood?"

Hal nodded and we all rose as the judge left. Sheriff Peterson paid the bail and we all meandered outside. "Hal is still staying with you, Sheriff?"

"Yes. I might have to hire another companion or my wife may just file for divorce."

"She's too good for her britches," Hal said. "I told you not to marry that city girl."

"Joy is too busy to be babysitting you. She has business to attend to."

"I don't need no damn babysitter you fool."

Trouble in Tawas

"I didn't mean it literally, Dad! You just need to behave yourself until we get you out of this fix."

"You believe me, son. Don't you? I swear it was all Mildred's idea, and I had nothing to do with Raul falling down those stairs. I swear he was fine when I saw him upstairs before we left that day."

"You're not being charged in connection with Raul's death. It looks like an accident."

Hal relaxed some as his shoulders drooped. "I'll try to behave, but the least you could do is find something for me to do. I like to whittle."

I couldn't imagine it wise to give Hal a knife, so I suggested, "How about a puzzle? I heard you loved to do puzzles when you were at the nursing home."

His eyes lit up, as did the sheriff's. "Great idea, Agnes. I hope you plan to find Mildred next. I sure would love to hear her side of the story."

"I had planned to, Peterson."

Sheriff Peterson and Hal left in a squad car, which left Andrew, El, and I to stand there, admiring the beautiful lake across US 23. "Do you want to go with us to Elsie Bradford's house, Andrew?"

He beamed. "It's about time I meet the old bird. You and El speak so highly of her."

"She's the gossip queen of East Tawas," I informed him.

"And not the only one in town," he winked.

El turned away like she had no idea of whom he was referring to. I, on the other hand, don't consider myself any more a gossip monger than anyone else in town. It was a small town after all.

We hopped back in the LX and I gave Andrew directions. Soon we were rumbling up Plank Road, heading out of town. Andrew turned up the drive that had a Victorian shaped mailbox. The cottage style house had bay windows, the newly hung siding was a robin egg blue. When we clamored up the sidewalk, I saw the 'No Smoking' sign alerting us that oxygen was in use.

I pushed the doorbell, and hid behind Andrew when I heard the sound of barking dogs. Since when did Elsie have a dog?

Elsie opened the door, oxygen tubing in her nostrils. "Hello. You said you wanted to meet my Andrew, right?"

"Well, I've seen him before, dear, but it's great to finally meet him officially. Come on in, but watch out for my oxygen cord."

We followed Elsie inside and I saw that the interior was the same as before, with all white walls and carpet, flowers positioned on end tables. Yup, it still looked like a funeral home to me.

"Come on into the dining room. I don't use the living room."

Lord, didn't I know it. I couldn't blame her for not wanting to mar her all white sofa and loveseat. I felt a little stab in my heart. I sure missed my house in the woods. Hopefully by the time this case was done, I'd be able to move in.

We piled into the room, and we each took a seat at the table while Elsie motioned to a woman standing in the corner, dressed in blue scrubs. "Bring us a pitcher of lemonade."

"But, Ms. Elsie, I'm only here to take your vital signs."

"Come now, dear. We're all thirsty. You don't want one of us dropping off, do you?"

El slapped her head, and said, "I feel about ready to fall out."

The woman rolled her eyes and disappeared into the other room, returning with the lemonade and glasses. "I'm on a tight schedule today."

Elsie dutifully held out an arm for the woman to place a cuff around, and with a whish, it inflated as the woman stared at the dial.

"That's not even a real blood pressure cuff," El said. "You can buy one of those yourself at any drug store."

The woman cocked her head. "I know that, but the company doesn't want to pay for a real one with a stethoscope."

"Then how are you going to listen to her lungs? With all the lemonade this one drinks, she might be overloaded with fluids."

"You tell her, Eleanor," Elsie said with a chuckle.

El wouldn't leave it alone. "Are you even a nurse?"

"No, ma'am. I'm a nursing care assistant."

"Don't ruin this for me, El," Elsie said. "This is the only company I have had recently."

I straightened in my chair. "What about your sister Mildred? Isn't she staying with you?"

Elsie sipped her lemonade and choked out, "No. I can barely tolerate her at family functions, which shouldn't be that much of a surprise to you, Aggie."

"I thought you were mad at me because of Mildred."

"Don't be silly. We've been friends far too long to let something like my sister come between us. I've missed our visits and our card parties."

I was taken aback by her admission. "Thanks for saying that, Elsie. I've missed you too."

Andrew smiled. "See, what did I tell you? And here you were worried."

"Well, I did fornicate with Mildred's husband years ago."

El slapped her knee. "Old news, dear."

"I agree," Elsie said. "I know how my sister can get sometimes, but since she began dating Hal Peterson, I thought she had turned over a new leaf. It's just awful what happened to Raul."

I rested the rim of my glass on my chin. "What did Mildred say happened to Raul?"

"Just that Raul was so cross with Hal that it was no wonder he fell down the stairs."

"I don't understand. How would Raul being cross with Hal result in him falling down the stairs?"

"Well, Hal pushed him of course."

"Is that what Mildred said?"

"Not in so many words, but she got her point across."

"Which means what?"

"That Hal and Raul were fighting on the stairs the day they left for Mt. Pleasant."

"Did Mildred witness the whole thing?"

"She said she went to wait in the car."

"So Mildred never saw anything other than an argument?"

"That's enough isn't it? Hal must have pushed him."

"Even if they were arguing that day, it doesn't mean he pushed him. There's no evidence to suggest Raul didn't accidentally fall down the stairs."

Elsie nodded. "I'm sure you're right, Aggie, but he stole Raul's credit card all the same."

"Yes, and Mildred knew that, but Hal claims it was her idea to steal Raul's card."

"My sister wouldn't do that. She might be a bit crazy, but she's not about to be involved in a theft."

"That remains to be seen, and why it's so important that I speak with your sister. Do you know where she's staying?"

"She's at the County Medical Facility for a few weeks. She's there for physical therapy."

"For what?"

"She bruised her hip and she's having a devil of a time walking."

"Bruised hip you say?" El asked. She stood, as did we all. We said our goodbyes and thanked Elsie for her information.

Once we were back in the LX, I blurted out, "I wonder how she bruised her hip?"

"Maybe you don't want to know," El said with a wink.

"Maybe she bruised it when she pushed Raul down the stairs?"

"Oh come now, Agnes," Andrew said. "How big was this Raul?"

"He was a big guy," El said. "But you know how strong crazy old bats can be."

"I know it sounds farfetched, but it's all we have to go on for now."

"I thought you had another suspect?" Andrew asked.

"We do," El admitted. "Harry Hunan."

"Is that his real name? It sounds like an alias of some sort."

"I thought that too, but he's married to a famous writer. S.S. Murphy. She writes erotica."

Andrew looked at me through the rearview mirror. "Figures, but what makes you think he was involved in Raul's mishap?"

"He was on Raul's Facebook page and also on Marie Sanchez's. We think it sounds like a worthwhile lead, since both of them are now dead. I think their deaths were made to look like accidents."

"For what possible motive?"

"We're not sure, but we found a deed to a house where the writer is living with her husband, Harry. She told us her husband owned the house."

"I'd like to take a look at that deed."

"I'll show you later, but right now I want to question Mildred."

"Okay, but I have a hard time believing she's involved in Raul's death. Have you considered whether his death was really an accident?"

"Yes, but my gut says otherwise."

"I understand, Aggie, but this might just be a waste of your time."

"Since when does your man call the shots?" El asked.

"He doesn't—"

Andrew cut in with, "I was just making an observation."

"Point taken, Andrew, but Aggie and I need to figure this out by ourselves. Maybe you should wait outside in the car."

Andrew expelled a breath. "Fine. I'll wait in the car."

He pulled into the County Medical Facility and El and I went inside. We inquired at the desk where we would find Mildred Winfree and the receptionist took us to a private room. "Maybe she'll cheer up with a little company."

Before either of us could question her, the receptionist took off down the long hallway.

I pushed the door open slightly and heard a loud shrill voice yell, "I told you to leave me alone!"

We walked in and I flipped on the light. Mildred was in the bed with the covers over her head. The room was sparsely furnished with a bed, dresser, and bedside table that held an uneaten tray of food.

Slowly the blankets came down. Mildred was dressed in brown slacks and shirt, tennis shoes on her feet. "Are you planning to go somewhere?" I asked Mildred.

"When third shift gets here, I'm outta here."

"You won't get far," Eleanor said. "All the doors have alarms on them."

"I know, but they can't catch us all."

"All, you mean you're not the only one escaping tonight?" I asked.

"Well, no. There's Helen Pocockie. She has Alzheimer's, or so they think."

I shifted to my good hip. "Oh really? She convinced you that she doesn't have it?"

"Oh she might have it, but Helen is more with it than they think and she sure keeps them on their toes. At one a.m., residents will open all the doors. There is no way they can catch us all."

Eleanor giggled. "Great plan, but it sounds dangerous. You should know most of the residents here would get hurt if they got outside."

Mildred sat up with a wince. "Who says?"

"Hal has dementia and look at what trouble he got into."

"We managed to get to Mt. Pleasant without incident, and if that fool hadn't lost all the money, we'd be sitting pretty right now."

"You can't keep it rolling forever. Even if you had won at the casino, the odds are stacked up against you."

"Ya," El added. "The House rules."

"I hate to admit you're right so I won't. Get lost you two before you mess up our plan."

"We'll talk about that later. For now, I want to ask you a few questions."

"Always the consummate investigators aren't you?"

"We try," El said. "Hal seemed upset."

"He hasn't heard from you. Didn't you tell him where you are?" I asked.

"I have my own problems. I can't be worrying about his. Plus, I heard he was arrested."

What a sweetheart. "He was, but he's out on bail."

"I see. Well, that's good and all, but I think I should find me a new beau. One who owns a yacht."

I smiled to myself. "Where are you planning to find one of those?"

"Not here in East Tawas," El said. "Most of those men are married, except for the young ones."

"Plenty of able-bodied men looking to date an older woman," Mildred said. "They like a woman with a steady income."

It took all of my efforts to not laugh outright. "You mean your social security checks, don't you dear?"

"I just love the direct deposits they do these days, but I won't get a red cent if I stay in this place."

"We have another question for you," El began. "We were led to believe that you were the one who decided to steal Raul's credit card."

"What? That old fool is trying to pin this on me? Sure I suggested it, but I was only joking. I had no idea he'd really go through with it."

"But you did know he was using the stolen card, so you're not blameless," I reminded her. "Maybe you should come clean and tell the police you were also involved."

"Agnes Barton, have you lost your mind?"

"Is that a rhetorical question?" El asked. "Because—"

"Are you insinuating I'm nuts, El?" I bellowed.

Mildred's eyes widened. "Girls, calm down before someone comes!"

There was a knock, and a nurse stood at the door. "Is everything alright in here? Mildred?"

"Of course. My friends were just mad when they saw the slop you were trying to feed me. They were just leaving."

I glared at Mildred. "She's right, we're leaving, but we'd like some privacy to say our goodbyes."

The nurse nodded and left, closing the door softly behind her.

"What happened between Raul and Hal that day you left?"

"They had an argument, but I waited outside."

"So you didn't want to get involved?"

"Raul and Hal always fought, it was a daily occurrence. Hal is quite stubborn at times, and Raul just wouldn't give us any time alone."

"I see. And then what happened?"

"Hal told me he had locked Raul in the upstairs bathroom. The door knob was broke and it fell off sometimes from the inside. And when it did, whoever was in the bathroom was stranded until someone came along to help out."

"Who's car did you take?"

"Raul's, but we left it in the Walmart parking lot and took the bus to Mt. Pleasant."

"Did you believe Hal's story about the bathroom?"

"Yes, no reason to think otherwise. Hal is incapable of harming a flea, despite his rough exterior. He was once a sheriff in Iosco County."

"I know. Thanks, Mildred, and good luck tonight."

She struggled to stand, but fell back and winced. "Ugh!"

I was shocked at her condition. "Can you walk?"

"Awww. Awwww. My hip hurts like the dickens."

"What happened to your hip?"

"I fell at my sisters. I tripped over her oxygen tubing."

I gave her a sympathetic glance and had a twinge of my own on my bad hip. "Maybe you should postpone your plan tonight."

"No way! I'll be okay. My car is parked in the parking lot."

"No it's not," Eleanor said. "We saw it back at your sister's house."

"So how are you planning to leave?"

"You could always give me a ride."

I shook my head. I couldn't believe she thought I'd help her out. "Take care, Mildred," I said as I left with Eleanor in tow.

I stared up the hall at the wheel chairs and walkers moving down the hall. I could not in good conscience let Mildred or her accomplices leave tonight from this facility, or any other night. It simply wasn't safe, and for that reason alone, I reported the plan to the receptionists. "Oh my! Oh my! Thanks for telling us. I'll put the staff on high alert."

I felt a pang of guilt at doing that to Mildred, but it was obvious that she was not in any condition to leave this facility just yet. With hard work, I was sure she'd be out soon.

Chapter Sixteen

I had barely made it out of bed the next morning when a rattled Leotyne knocked on the door. I threw open the door and she pulled me outside. "Woman on the beach is talking bad about that sheriff of yours. She has brought a vicious bird with her!"

Martha jumped up, as did El, who had spent the night. We met outside once we were dressed, then made our way for the beach. Mrs. Barry stood in the middle of a group of women. Her friends, the bird sisters, were there too, cackling like birds. Was that what Leotyne was talking about?

"Crazy lady. Crazy lady," a bird screeched.

My eyes widened when I saw a red, green, and black McCaw on the beach, no less. He was standing on a perch that was on a picnic table.

"You better listen to that bird," I said. "Mrs. Barry is a crazy lady!"

Mrs. Barry whirled with her teeth bared. "You!" she screeched.

We circled one another, both of us breathing heavily.

"What are you carrying on about now?"

"How unfit that sheriff is. His father is under arrest as we speak."

"No, he was bailed out yesterday."

"It doesn't matter. He's a lawbreaker!"

"No, he was once a sheriff in Iosco County and a good one at that. He was a well-respected sheriff when he tackled the Robinson Murder case. Unfortunately it turned cold, but that man never for a moment forgot about that case."

"Aggie and I solved that case with the sitting sheriff's help, not to mention Trooper Sales." El said, pointing a bony finger in Mrs. Barry's face. "This woman would have you believe that Sheriff Peterson doesn't deserve to be re-elected, but we know better. If Clay Barry is elected, Agnes and I won't be allowed to solve crimes. What do you think about that?" El asked the group of beachgoers.

"What do I care," a man said. "I don't even live here."

"Then why are you speaking?" El asked.

"That would be a shame," Rosa Lee Hill said. "Agnes convinced me to stop growing marijuana and I now have respectable potpourri business."

I smiled. I hadn't known I had gotten through to her. "Thanks, Rosa. Where are your boys these days?"

"They are at summer camp."

Sure the Hill boys were. They were part of the Michigan Militia. Those are two boys you'd want on your side.

"I don't know where this Clay character came from, but he's not the type of man we need for sheriff," Dorothy Alton said. "He's been hitting on our granddaughter Sally. And he doesn't take no for an answer."

Mrs. Barry's face turned fire engine red. "Take that back!" She raised a bony fist, "Or else!"

Boom... pow... Mrs. Barry fell to the beach with a thump.

I stared at Mrs. Barry and then to Dorothy, who smiled like a champ. "I can't have you girls put out of commission. Who knows when our next crime wave will happen?"

"I sure hope you girls figure out what really happened to Raul Perez," Frank Alton said. "And that poor girl at the beach. Do you think the crimes are connected?"

"We're working on solving the crimes, but sure could use some help. Does anyone know about a Hummer seen in the area recently?"

"I've seen one over at Walmart," Dorothy said. "It's just crazy to drive a gas guzzler like that these days with the price of gas."

I had to agree with that. "When was that?"

"Yesterday."

I thanked Dorothy and the others and left before Mrs. Barry found her tongue. I was glad this time around I wasn't the one tussling with Barry. I was too old to be fighting with anyone. Besides, it takes too long for bruises to heal.

"Mother, would you wait up?" Martha said. "That was so cool of your friends, sticking up for you."

"Especially when some of them weren't friends, like Dorothy Alton."

Trouble in Tawas

"Aww come on. You sure got along with her in Florida."

"That's true. She was quite helpful then, and El and I did save her life."

Martha smiled. "I just love all you old birds getting along. Next thing you know, you'll patch things up with Mildred Winfree."

I waved to Leotyne and sat down at the picnic table. "I doubt that. She's at the County Medical Facility, and I told them she was planning to escape last night."

Martha frowned, but then said, "Maybe she won't figure out it was you that told."

"I sure hope not."

"It's a good thing you did, telling them I mean. Old people shouldn't be allowed to roam the streets."

I fanned myself, as it was hot already. "Oh, thanks a lot!"

"Don't read too much into it, Mother. If she's in there, it must be for a good reason."

"Yes, she took a fall at her sister's house."

"See, she needs to be there for awhile. Maybe she'll get better soon and she can go home."

"Problem is that I don't know where home really is for her. Elsie didn't sound like she cared to have her staying with her."

"Probably all talk. I'm sure it will all work out."

"Hopefully." I sat in silence, until Martha asked, "I hope you don't mind if I tag along with you and Eleanor today? I can be of help on your case."

I smiled like a cat, until Mr. Tinkles began to yap up a storm. I let him outside on his chain, and asked Martha, "Do you know who S.S. Murphy is?"

"You mean the erotica writer?" she squealed. "I heard she was in town. She has a book signing at the library today."

"Sounds like a good time to pay her another visit."

"What do you mean another visit?"

"We stopped by where she's staying in town."

Martha gave me a hug and ran off, presumably to change. She returned dressed in white leggings with a yellow midriff top, high-heeled sandals on her feet. Even though she was in her forties, her abs were tight. She worked out every night doing crunches and squats. If

Martha planned on dating men half her age, she needed a rockin' body to boot. I still can't understand what possesses her to strut around town looking like she was ripped from the seventies, or like a hooker, as some thought. I have since given up on lecturing others how to dress.

We took the station wagon to El's and waited until she surfaced, wearing lavender capris and a matching blouse. Her hair had a real shine to it, with glitter spray applied. "Wow, El. You're going way out for the book signing."

"Well, she *is* my favorite author."

"Not me," I admitted. "I'm more of a cozy mystery buff, especially books with senior aged characters."

"Maybe someday someone will write a book about us, Aggie."

I nodded as I led the way outside. "I sure like the sound of that, but nobody would ever think we're believable."

"Why not? Just because we're old doesn't make us incapable of solving crimes. Sure we get aches and pains, but it never stops us when we're on a case."

We hopped into the car, and I added, "You got that one right!"

Ten minutes later I was on Sawyer Street at the East Tawas Library. My eyes widened when I saw the huge line that had formed outside the mostly brick library.

El's shoulders slumped. "We'll be here all day."

"It looks that way, but maybe I can work us in."

I went back to the car and returned with a quad cane I had forgotten I had left in the station wagon a month ago. At that time I was having trouble with my hip, but luckily it was a short-lived inconvenience, but I needed a cane for support. My hip has been aching for years, but I wanted to forego surgery as long as possible.

I limped my way toward the door despite the odd glances thrown my way. El followed my cue and did the best impression of an invalid I had ever seen. She clung to the doorway. "Oh... oh!" she wailed.

"I hope you're not thinking about cutting in the line," a young woman said. "The line starts back there," she said, pointing a bony finger behind her.

"If we do that, we'll drop off for sure," I whined. "Let us go first. I promise we won't take more than a few minutes to speak with S.S. Murphy."

"So you're gonna pull the 'I'm old and should get extra privilege's' card?" she sneered. "Why do women your age even read erotica?"

"I'll have you know young lady, it's been around longer than you were a twinkle in your parent's eye," El said sweetly. "What would your grandmother think of you speaking to your elders this way?"

"My granny is in a nursing home where she belongs."

El's face turned a shade of red, and I pushed her ahead of me before she put a hurting on this woman. As it was, I wanted to slap her smug face, but decided it simply wasn't worth the trouble it would cause. I sure didn't want to get arrested again.

I went through the door, and Melinda the librarian rolled her eyes, but led us straight to where the author had a table set up, with her books on easels. Behind the table was a huge sign with the picture of her recent book, Highland Honey. The image was of a young man with bare chest who only wore a kilt, whereas the woman wore a blue dress pulled down enough to reveal ample cleavage. One could say it was a traditional bodice ripper cover. It was so out of place with contemporary romance taking center stage these days.

When S.S. Murphy strode through the back door, she was dressed sensibly in crème colored slacks, with a satin button-up blouse that revealed her creamy skin beneath. The curls of her long dark hair rested on her shoulders. Her blue eyes widened in recognition as she asked us, "Are you here for the book signing?"

"Yes," El gushed, obviously star struck, but it wasn't every day that you saw a bestselling author first hand.

"My book is $14.99," she said, indicating the book on the table.

"I already have that book," El said as she pulled it from her purse.

I reached into my wallet and bought a book, and with a quaint smile I asked, "We'd like to ask you more questions if you don't mind."

"Not now," El said. "Please, sign my book. My name is Eleanor Mason."

A small sharpie pen was applied to El's book and it was handed back. "I'm too busy right now, but if you'd buy me dinner later, I'd be happy to answer your questions."

"How about Hidden Cove? They have the best lake perch in town."

S.S. Murphy's lip curved down into a frown. "I'm not that much of a fish lover."

"They also cook a mean steak," El quickly added. "What time is good for you?"

"How about eight o'clock?"

We agreed to meet at that time, and I had S.S. sign the book I bought for my daughter, who I knew didn't have the funds for a book of her own.

***

A quarter after eight, El, Martha and I were seated on the balcony of Hidden Cove. It was still light enough at this point that the deck lights weren't needed. When S.S. Murphy strolled toward us, she stumbled briefly and nearly fell sideways, catching herself on the table next to us. She laughed and apologized to the younger couple seated at the table. I got up and held out a chair for the author, hoping she'd not head straight to the floor, as I could smell the whisky on her breath.

"Sorry I'm late. I got lost after I left the liquor store," she slurred. "I mean grocery store."

She was dressed the same as earlier, but her clothing looked rumpled now. She tucked her hair behind her ears and my eyes widened when I noted the huge diamond rings on her fingers. She must have noticed my glance, as she announced, "They're not real, dear. I bought these knock offs on the Home Shopping Network."

"Oh really?" El said. "Doesn't your husband buy you jewelry?"

"My husband Harry is only good for one thing—"

"Good luvin'," El suggested.

"I wish. Let's just say he's not anything like the men I write about in my books. More of a limp noodle."

Too much information, but at least she was talking. I offered the menu and she ordered a nineteen dollar steak and a long island ice tea, but I suspected she could do without any more to drink.

"I so know what you mean," El said with a wink. "Men are never who they say they are. He can't be all bad, he did buy the beach house on Lake Huron, right?"

She frowned. "That's what worries me. I don't know how on earth he managed to do that. He has run my credit into the gutter."

I gasped. "Aww, you poor dear. Surely he has a job."

"Sponging off me is his full-time job, but lately he assured me he had something in the works. I just hope it's not another stripper."

"He cheats on you?" El asked with a sharp intake of breath. "He's obviously a loser. Maybe you should file for divorce."

"I can't or he'll get half of my royalty checks."

"Didn't you have him sign a prenup?"

"Nope, my books hadn't started to really sell until after I married the bum. This is the one time I wish I had listened to my mother."

Martha laughed loudly, "Don't say that. I'm sure you just thought he was somebody he wasn't. It's easy for us women to fall for the wrong man."

I glared at Martha. Would it hurt her to think that a mother sometimes knows what she's talking about? "My daughter is right," I added, and then moved my drink so the waitress could put down my perch I had ordered before S.S. Murphy arrived.

We waited until we each were given our food before we said anything else. Martha and El had each ordered smothered chicken. "Things will work out, hopefully, but what makes you think your husband was seeing a stripper? Has he done it before?"

"Yes, too many times to count."

"Does your husband own a Hummer?" I asked, hoping it didn't sound too abrupt of a question.

"No, a black Impala."

"Do you know anyone who owns a Hummer?"

She forked in some steak, chewed, swallowed and then said, "No. You don't think my husband is involved in a crime, I hope."

"We just don't know yet. We're looking for a man who drives a Hummer, but we think we saw your husband at Fuzzy's Ice Cream Shop not long ago. Do you happen to have his picture with you?"

S.S. Murphy pulled out her wallet and flashed Harry's picture. It was the same one he had on his Facebook page. "Thanks. Did you know Raul Perez?"

"The man they found dead in town? Why no. Why?"

"We were led to believe he had business dealings with Raul is all. I just wish we could talk to your husband."

"I'll try to work that out, but he didn't come home last night. I truthfully don't know where he could be."

"Does he carry a smart phone, one with GPS tracking?" I asked.

"He does. I'll have his phone tracked in the morning."

"If you could give us his number I could save you the trouble. I'm sure the sheriff could check it out for us."

El's eyes were round as saucers. "I'm not sure he'll help us out."

"We'll simply tell the sheriff that his wife is concerned."

S.S. drank her drink faster that I thought she should, but I kept my lips zipped. "I hope you can back up our story if the sheriff asks," I suggested.

"Sure thing. I know I should be more concerned than I am about his whereabouts, but he's disappeared on me before, sometimes for weeks."

"You shouldn't put up with that!" El spat.

"I know, but I guess I'm just thankful to have a man in my life. Once you get over the age of forty its slim pickings."

"Don't say that, S.S.," El said with sympathy. "I'm over eighty and I have a man. If I can do it, so can you."

"I like how Harry lets me write, but perhaps that was a mistake on my part. I gave him too much freedom, obviously."

"Don't worry. I promise we'll find him for you. Maybe it's not as dire as it seems," I tried to reassure her.

"I hope you're right. I'm sorry I was so cross with you the other day at the house. I just hadn't expected strangers to be on the property."

"And there's nobody stranger than my mother and her odd friend," Martha said with a twinkle in her eye.

Neither El nor I were about to give Martha the satisfaction of a smart come back. When we had finished dinner and our drinks, I escorted S.S. Murphy outside and into the station wagon. No way did I want her wrapping her car around a tree on my conscience.

Chapter Seventeen

Bright and early the next morning, El and I were seated in the sheriff's office waiting for him to retrieve coffee. I was thinking more for him than us, since he didn't know yet why we were here. He precariously carried the cups to his desk and I jumped up to help least I lose my first chance at a cup of brew. I took a sip and smiled. "Not bad at all."

"The new girl, Janice, makes a great cup of coffee."

I had noticed the vibrant young lady who manned the counter. "Maybe I should close your door," I suggested.

"Oh," he raised a brow. "It's going to be one of those kinds of conversations?"

"Yes."

"What do you need me to do this time?"

"Run a GPS on a cell phone."

"For who?"

"Harry Hunan. I have his number here." I handed him a slip of paper.

"I need probable cause."

"He's married to the author S.S. Murphy and she told us he hasn't returned home."

"Then why isn't she here?"

"Nursing a hangover no doubt."

"I see. I need her to verify he's missing before I run a check. I have to watch my back, you know."

I pulled out my cell and found S.S. Murphy's number she had given me last night and the sheriff dialed the number as I recited it. "This is Sheriff Peterson here. Is your husband missing?"
He paused. "I see. Has he shown up yet?" He hung up and turned to his laptop and keyed in the number I gave him. "I have enough probable cause to run a check. She'll be along shortly to file a missing person's report."

Peterson raised a brow. "I know I shouldn't be telling you this, but he's at the Northland Cabins. I'll be heading out there now, you can follow, but... let me be clear that you will stand back. Is that understood?"

"Of course, Sheriff. He's a person of interest in Raul Perez's accident. We had hoped to question him, but it just wasn't in the cards."

"Story of my life." He leaned back in his leather chair and hauled his bulky body upward, making tracks for the door with us in hot pursuit. When we arrived at the Northland Cabins five short minutes later, we parked alongside the sheriff and waited as he walked to the cabin and knocked. When nobody answered, he flagged down the cleaning lady who was pushing her cart past. Keys rattled as she unlocked the door and Peterson disappeared inside. He stuck his head out fast-like and nodded at us. With that cue El and I left the station wagon and walked inside the cabin.

My eyes panned left to right as we entered the cabin with the knotty pine walls and went into the bedroom. On the top of the rose bedspread was the body of a man. When I approached the bed, I saw it was indeed Harry Hunan. From the gray cast appearance of his skin and open unseeing eyes, I knew him to be dead. On the bed there was an empty pill bottle and a note scrawled with a red pen. It read as follows: *I killed Raul Perez and Maria Sanchez in an act of passion. I was having an affair with Maria and found out she was also sleeping with Raul, and I killed them both and made it look like an accident. I want to apologize to my loving wife and to the family of both Raul and Maria.*

"I don't get it," El said. "This seems like a set up."

"I have to agree with you, El. Someone went to a lot of trouble to make this look like a suicide."

"Now listen here," Peterson said. "For all we know he really did kill himself."

"Why would he mention Raul and Maria when both deaths were ruled accidental?"

"Perhaps he didn't know that," Peterson suggested, "and it was too much of a burden for him."

"I don't believe that for a minute. Pills are not how men usually

Trouble in Tawas

take their own life," I insisted.

"No?" El asked. "Then how do they usually do it?"

"Guns tend to be the preferred method."

"Or hanging," Peterson added. "The coroner will do a toxicology to determine if pills were indeed the cause of death."

I stared at the pill bottle without picking it up. "This is oxycodone and it looks like Harry had a prescription for it."

"It doesn't look like there are any visible wounds, so how would somebody force Harry to take the pills? Would they still be in his stomach?" El asked.

"Probably absorbed into his system," I said. "Right, Sheriff?"

"Depending on how long ago he took the pills."

El stared at the nightstand. "What if he was drugged?"

"Well, there's no glasses in here. Maybe in the other room." I led the way and into the kitchen, spotting two glasses. "These glasses should be tested for the presence of drugs."

"Why on earth would Harry take the pills out here?" El asked.

"It looks like he might have had company, there are two glasses. I believe the crime scene was staged."

"Anyone in their right mind would get rid of any evidence, but I'll be sure to have those glasses checked."

"Oh? Are you investigating this crime?"

"Of course, Agnes. Why would you think otherwise?"

I bit down on my fingernail. "It's just that Harry's note claims he killed Raul and since your father was involved, I thought it might be better if you stayed off this case."

"That's not going to happen, Agnes. This is one crime I want to get to the bottom of, for all of our sakes."

My eyes widened. "So you don't believe it's a suicide either?"

"Not a chance, but I know it's never good to jump to conclusions. It might bite us all in the ass. I'm calling this one in, and I think you two had best skedaddle before—"

Trooper Sales' frame filled the doorway. "Before I show up, don't you mean? What are they doing here?"

"H-How did you get here so soon?"

"I happened to be driving by when the call came in from Peterson," Sales informed us.

It figures! "We're working a case and it led us here," I said. "I guess our red herring is dead again."

"Red herring, eh? And here you are in the middle of it again. Please leave so I can assist the sheriff here. I don't need any guff from either of you. This is a police investigation, one where your opinions aren't welcomed," Sales added.

"Of all the nerve. We're practically family."

"I know. Another reason you shouldn't be here. This is the last thing I need right now."

"Well, go ahead and investigate all you want. El and I have all the information we need."

"It looks like this case might be wrapped up sooner than we had hoped," Peterson said. "I appreciate all your help. Really."

Sales' brow furrowed. "Help? How were they helping you?"

"I hired them, if you need to know."

Trooper Sales face turned red. "For what?"

"They were working on clearing my dad's name."

"Clearing his name how?"

"My dad never murdered Raul."

"Of course he didn't. Raul's death was ruled an accident."

"Harry Hunan is dead in the bedroom and his suicide note states he killed both Raul Perez and Maria Sanchez. So much for accidents," I clarified.

"We believe the suicide was a setup," El added. "Isn't that right, Aggie?"

"Yes, and we'll happily be leaving now to find the real killer."

Trooper Sales went into the bedroom and I merely shrugged as El and I went towards the door, until Peterson stopped us dead in our tracks. "Be careful, Agnes. The last thing I need to worry about is the two of you."

El and I were in the station wagon by the time more cops cars tore into the parking lot. I backed up and narrowed my eyes at the flashing lights. It was more than I cared to visualize. I drove to the beach house S.S. Murphy was staying at. I knew it wasn't my place, but I felt it was my duty to tell the author about her husband's demise. I'm sure I'd take the heat later, but at this point, I didn't care what Trooper Sales thought I should or shouldn't do.

"Who do you think set up Harry's suicide?" El asked. "His wife?"

"That's a possibility I suppose, but I just don't see her that way, and we were with her last night, remember?"

"Yes, but she made her husband sound like a total loser, and she stood to lose a considerable sum if Harry divorced her."

"True, but that lady is no more a murderer than you are."

"We should be careful, like the sheriff said," El suggested.

"We will. S.S. just has no reason to want Raul and Maria dead."

"The note said they were having an affair and Harry was involved with Maria." Wham! She slammed a fist against the dash. "Plenty of motive."

"We'll give her the news and keep our options open."

"What we really need to do is read her expressions. That should tell us all we need to know. If she overreacts she might be guilty."

"I thought you were one of her fans, El?"

"I am, but that doesn't mean I should turn a blind eye if she's guilty."

***

Ten minutes later we rapped on the door of the beach house where S.S. Murphy was staying while she was in town. Her husband owned the house, she claimed, but we knew better. According to the deed, Raul Perez owned it, with Maria Sanchez as a beneficiary.

Sasha Murphy never answered the door and I peered through the windows, but didn't see any movement within. "Maybe she's not home," I said.

"Let's go around back. She could be outside getting a suntan," El suggested.

"Or nursing a hangover."

We carefully walked around the house, playing on the side of caution. There were some ruts and holes in the lawn—and dog feces—the last thing I needed on my shoes. Sasha Murphy was indeed on a lounge chair, dressed in a white bikini, soaking up the rays. On a table next to her was a glass with clear liquid, filled with ice. *Is she drinking again this soon?*

"Hello there," I called out.

Sasha lifted her sunglasses and faintly smiled. "Oh, hello girls. Did we make plans for today?"

"You mean you don't remember?" I asked in a serious tone.

"I-I don't remember anything after I left the book signing. I might have had too much to drink."

"You definitely did," El said. "You were slouched up by the time you met us at Hidden Cove."

"Sorry about that. I was in a fit yesterday about my husband Harry. The sheriff called me earlier. Did he track Harry's cell?"

Whisking a stray hair from my face, I said, "Yes he did. That's why we're here."

"Let me guess. You found him at a motel room with another woman, right?"

"We found him all right, but—"

"Spit it out, old girl. I can take whatever you have to say. I know all about Harry's dalliances."

I pursed my lips, and then as gently as I could I told her, "We found your husband at one of the cabins at Northland cabins... he's dead, dear. It appears to be a suicide."

Sasha's sunglasses clattered to the ground and her mouth gaped open. "Oh my, that can't be. My Harry would never take his life."

"So he's never been depressed or talked about suicide?"

"No. I need to call my agent. This won't be good when the press gets ahold of this." She picked up her cell and I took it from her hand. "We have more questions. I know this was a shock, but we really need to know if Harry was having an affair for sure?"

She bit down on her fist. "He's been preoccupied lately, but he told me it had something to do with a business deal."

"Who was he doing business with?"

"I don't know."

"So there wasn't a woman you were aware of that he was seeing behind your back?"

"Do you know something I don't?"

"Maybe, but if you can't tell us the name of a woman he was seeing, I'm not sure I should tell you."

"Tell her, Agnes."

"Maybe we should wait for the sheriff," I said.

Sasha took ahold of my shirt. "Please tell me."

"Do you know Maria Sanchez?"

"The woman who drowned on the beach, the one they were talking about on the news?"

"Yes."

"No. Was my husband having an affair with that woman? It might explain his suspicious behavior of late."

"Suspicious behavior?"

"He has been quiet since Maria was found dead at the beach. If he was indeed having an affair with this woman, it's no wonder he started clamming up. He barely spoke to me and he seemed so distracted. I couldn't get through to him."

I noted that Sasha had so far not shed a tear. "There was a suicide note left at the cabin. Harry wrote that he was having an affair with Maria Sanchez and that so was Raul Perez. And he killed both of them, making it look like an accident."

"How awful. I'm shocked that my husband would kill anyone."

El stepped up and grabbed a tissue, dotting her eyes. "It was so awful finding your husband like that. We don't believe he killed himself at all."

I nodded. "It looks like a setup. Did you leave last night after we dropped you off?"

She sat upright. "You saw me last night. I was a wreck. I wasn't in any kind of condition to go anywhere, and my car was left at Hidden Cove, remember?"

That got my attention. "That's the strange part. You just said a few minutes ago that you were too drunk to remember what you did last night. And now you want us to believe you never left the house last night, but how about the night before? At this point, we have no idea how long your husband was dead, but the sheriff recovered two glasses at the crime scene."

"Yes!" El shouted. "Were you there yesterday or the night before?"

"No! I haven't seen my husband for over three days. I told you that!"

"No. You told us he just hadn't come home the night before. For all we know you found out where he was shacked up and you decided to get rid of him. You'd look like the sympathetic widow who lost her husband to suicide. You might even get more book sales."

"Why on earth would I do that?"

"Because he made a fool of you. You might have known all about Maria Sanchez. You already told us he'd get a substantial amount if he divorced you."

"You are crazy," her eyes shifted to Eleanor. "You're both crazy. I'm looking at damage control no matter the outcome when the press finds out my husband is dead. Are you suggesting I killed Maria too, or Raul Perez? I'd have no reason to want Raul dead, and is this how you see me, as a cold blooded killer capable of killing three people and staging the crimes to look like accidents, or a suicide in Harry's case?"

"She has a point, Aggie. Why kill Raul Perez?"

"Because Raul owned this house, and not your husband, with Maria Sanchez as the beneficiary."

"Harry owns this house! I'm sure he does."

"Why, because he told you so? There has to be a reason he had Raul buy the house instead."

El patted Sasha's hand. "Please tell us why Harry would have someone else buy the house and lie to you about it."

"I don't know... unless—"

"Unless what?"

"He gambles, but he promised me he gave it all up. He assured me he had."

"You might want to check out his credit score before you make that kind of claim... once a gambler always a gambler, unless he got help. Well, did he?"

"He told me he did, but do you have proof that this house was bought by Raul?"

I pulled out the deed and handed it over to Sasha. "I c-can't believe this. Harry lied to me again!" Sasha ran into the house with us in tow. She pulled out her laptop and clicked her way onto the credit check site. Harry's credit score was displayed at 410. "That bastard! I don't know about any of these credit cards." She checked her own credit score and found it just as bad. "I-I can't believe he's done this to me! He's gotten credit cards in my name and they are all maxed out. He's ruined me!"

"When is the last time you checked you bank account? Has he taken any money out of your accounts without your knowledge?"

Sasha checked, and her head slumped to her laptop. "There's over a hundred thousand missing!" Tears dripped from her eyes onto her desktop. "I've been misled, cheated on, and now, stolen from by my own husband. What else can happen?"

I knew it's never a good thing to say, because in my opinion things can always get worse. "I'm sorry, dear, and I emphasize with you. El and I will continue to investigate this case. I sure hope we can dig up something that will explain this. Who besides you would want Harry dead? You have no idea who he was doing business with?"

"No, I swear," she said as she threw herself into my arms. "Please believe me. I had nothing to do with this!"

I pushed her back. "Don't worry. We'll find out what really happened." I retrieved the deed and placed it back in my bag for safekeeping. "Please don't tell the sheriff we told you about your husband before he had a chance to. We'll do our best to find out the truth, and if we are arrested, we'll never be able to do it." I frowned and asked one more question, "One more question though. Why was Harry prescribed Oxycodone?"

"Harry has a bad back. He's been on it awhile, why?"

"An empty pill bottle was found on the bed next to him," El said.

Sasha nodded and we left in a roar with a trail of dust in our wake.

Chapter Eighteen

When we rolled back into the campground, Andrew was waiting alongside Martha. Mr. Tinkles was on the chain and they were chatting about something. Their faces lit up at our approach. When we met them on the porch, Martha shouted, "Sophia and Bill Sales are getting married!"

"What? When?"

"Sophia called after you left this morning. Bill proposed last night. Isn't it great?"

"Yes, but he didn't mention anything at the crime scene this morning."

Andrew's eyes widened. "What crime scene?"

"The author S.S. Murphy's husband, Harry Hunan, was found dead at the Northland Cabins. It's an apparent suicide, but I don't believe Harry killed himself. I think the crime scene was set up."

"That's what you always think, Aggie," Andrew said. "You have to admit that you might be wrong this time around."

"No way," El said. "Harry had a gambling problem, and he had Raul Perez buy a beach house for him so his wife wouldn't find out about it."

"Actually El, I wonder if Harry gave that money to Maria for safekeeping and she in turn gave it to Raul, her lover, who then bought the beach house."

"So you believe this Maria duped Harry?" Andrew asked.

"Yes, both Maria and Raul did. Of course Harry didn't find that out until later."

El nodded. "Okay, so Harry had the keys to beach house and he never knew it wasn't in Maria's name?"

"No, and I don't believe this had anything to do with a gambling debt. Harry figured if Maria bought the beach house, there was no way his wife could get any part of it."

"If Raul bought the house, then why did Harry even have the keys?" Andrew asked.

"Isn't it obvious?" El said. "They were buying their time, but I guess they were the ones out of options."

"Exactly. I don't think Maria ever intended to stay with Harry. He was married after all."

Andrew rubbed the back of his neck. "So you're saying that Harry stole money from his own wife and gave it to his mistress?"

"What does the writer have to say for herself?" Martha asked.

"She thought her husband owned the house, and that's not all, Raul owned the house and Maria Sanchez was the beneficiary. Maybe someone offed them both to take the property."

"Someone besides Harry?" Andrew asked, scratching his head. I handed the deed to Andrew and he took it inside to look it over. "Raul Perez and Maria Sanchez are the only names listed. The only person to benefit would have to be related to Maria Sanchez, a child if she had any, or parents... or brothers and sisters if there are any. If not, the estate would go to the state."

"This certainly puts a wrench in the plan. Harry's suicide note said that he was having an affair with Maria Sanchez, but that she was also sleeping with Raul Perez. At first I thought S.S. Murphy might have set up her husband's death, but now, it just makes no sense. She wouldn't benefit from the house if it goes into probate. I've checked her online profile and she isn't related to either Raul Perez or Maria Sanchez. I think whoever did this wanted both Raul's and Maria's deaths to look like they were murdered by Harry Hunan, who then supposedly committed suicide."

"To what end, Mother?" Martha asked.

"Whoever did this knew we wouldn't give up on this case. They wanted to put an end to our investigating for once and all."

"Fat chance that," El said. "I think Maria has some family in town... relatives who found out about the deed for the property. We found it in the ceiling of Maria's El Camino while it was in the impound yard."

"How did you do that?" Andrew asked.

"You don't want to know," Martha said with a roll of her eyes.

Andrew handed the deed back to me. "I agree with you there, but how do you plan to find out if Maria had any family in town, Aggie?"

"We're resourceful is how. We'll ask Sheriff Peterson," I said with a nod.

***

Later in the day I was waiting in the parking lot of Fuzzy's when the sheriff's car pulled up. He rolled his window and I approached the car, confident he'd help me. "Hello, Sheriff. I had hoped you'd come."

His brow furrowed. "What is it this time, Agnes? I hope you know Trooper Sales chastised me for allowing you at the last crime scene."

"So you do agree it was a crime scene?"

"We're waiting for the toxicology reports, which will be a few weeks, but I think it looks fishy."

I handed the deed to the sheriff. "I found this in Maria's El Camino at the impound yard."

"How? You're too old to scale the fence."

"I'd rather not say."

"I think I'll have to talk with Ralph. He should know better than to let anyone in that yard."

I sure didn't want to get Ralph in trouble. "El's Caddy was impounded, remember?"

"Yes, but it was picked up before the El Camino ever hit that lot."

Peterson doesn't miss anything! "I lied and told him I lost my wallet and searched the El Camino, if you need to know."

"So you interfered with police business again, and took what might be vital evidence to the Maria Sanchez case?"

"I didn't mean to, but you cops thought it was just a drowning."

"That's not true. Someone down at the news is releasing the wrong information. We thought it was wrong from the start. There wasn't any water in her lungs and the toxicology report came back that she had Oxycodone in her system, like enough to kill her."

"The same drug that was found at Harry Hunan's suicide?"

"Yes, and that's not all. It was also found in Raul Perez's bloodstream. It would have been enough to impair him... enough that he could be easily pushed to his death down a flight of steps, or so we suspect. All of this information came to light recently. See, us cops aren't as dumb as you think. We're doing our job."

"Can you run a check to find out if Maria Sanchez had any children in the area? They stand to inherit the house on Lake Huron."

"I'll look into that and thanks for the deed, but as far as I'm concerned you two are off the case. We'll wrap up the case from here on out. Relax and chill out on the beach like the rest of the old folks in town."

I sighed. "You won't let us take a tiny peek? I swear I won't tell anyone you did."

He shook his head. "Not happening, Agnes. Back away from the car so I can leave, and I hear congratulations are in order. Trooper Sales will be a great addition to your family. Maybe you can bug him in the future and leave me alone."

Before I had a chance to speak, I spotted Mrs. Barry stuck to the glass door of Fuzzy's. We waved to the sheriff and walked inside, elbowing Mrs. Barry on our way. "Sorry," I said with a smile.

"What were you talking to the sheriff about out there?"

"Oh, nothing much. He wanted to make sure we still planned to vote for him is all."

"He's gonna lose, you know. My son—"

My eyes widened when I saw Clay Barry, the candidate, grabbing Sally Alton's round buttocks. I was livid. I ran over there to her aid and shoved him back. He lost his balance and fell to the floor. "Some candidate for sheriff you are! You're already assaulting young women."

"Aw, I was not. She likes it when I do that," he winked.

Sally's hands flew to her hips and her mouth slacked open. "I most certainly do not! I told you to keep your hands to home the last time you were here!"

Chairs flew across the room, and two very tall and bulky men with blond hair stood with fists at the ready. It was none other than Curt and Curtis Hill, Rosa Lee's boys. Clay tried to get up, but kept sliding to the floor as patrons pummeled him with ice cream. Curt finally lifted him off the ground by the scuff of his neck, Clay's toes barely scraping the floor.

Mrs. Barry screamed at the top of her lungs. "Somebody stop this! He's going to be the next sheriff in Iosco County."

"No, dead men can't be sheriff," Curt threatened.

Clay's face was near purple when I finally said, "Let the man go before you kill him in a room full of witnesses."

Boom... Clay fell to the floor and gasped for air. Mrs. Barry flew to her son and unbuttoned his shirt. "You people are animals."

"Nope," Curtis spat on Clay. "My brother here is kinda sweet on Sally, and you ought to treat a lady with respect around this town, unless you want to be spitting teeth out."

"I'm calling the cops," Mrs. Barry said with gnashed teeth.

"Go ahead," I said. "Anyone see anything? Not me. How about you, Eleanor?"

"Not a thing. I was staring at the menu board. I think I'll get something different today."

Mrs. Barry punched in the numbers on her phone, but Clay knocked the phone from her mother's hand. "Are you crazy, Mom? You heard them! You want those fellas to kill me?"

"They don't have a right to treat you that way. You're gonna be the new sheriff in town."

"Not in this town I'm not. I'm withdrawing from the race. This town is full of crazies!"

"I'd be careful what you said in an ice cream parlor filled with crazies, as you say," I winked. "It wouldn't hurt to apologize to Sally here."

"Don't bother," Sally said. "I just want this trash out of here." She motioned to the Hill boys. "Take out the trash!"

Mrs. Barry helped her son up and out of Fuzzy's before the Hill brothers had a chance to move. "It's like I always say, you always want the Hill boys on your side."

"Thanks, Curt," Sally said, her face redder than I had ever seen it. Maybe Sally was a little sweet on Curt too.

Sally scooped up a banana split for El and a pineapple sundae for me as usual, and we ate our treats seated next to the Hill boys. We ate in silence, both of us on the same team. Who knew I'd be so comfortable sitting next to Curtis and Curt? They both had trouble with the law in the past and had put folks in town on edge. All I knew was my feeling for them had taken a serious change. I adored Rosa Lee to death, and she had herself a couple of good boys despite what some might think.

El and I said our goodbyes, and as we neared the door, I saw a black Hummer roll past. I gasped. "Eleanor, there is a Hummer in town."

"Sure is. They almost drove me off the road," I heard a male voice say. When we turned, it was none other than Mr. Wilson and a blond petite girl of twenty. "When did you get here, Wilson?" I asked.

"About five minutes ago. You and El were so into your desserts that Millicent and I didn't want to disrupt you." Mr. Wilson was dressed in gray work clothes, like he had worn when he was working, all those years ago. "Hello, Peaches," he greeted Eleanor and made the introductions.

El gave him a quick hug. "We have to be going now, but I'll give you a call tomorrow. Aggie and I are on a case. We have us a Hummer to track down."

"I see. Well, be careful girls. I'd hate to get my shotgun outta storage."

We nodded and then we were out the door. When I hopped into the station wagon, I gave El a beaming smile. "It's looks like we're both complete again. Your man is in town and my man is back in town."

"Complete? Are you kidding me? Since when did either of us need a man to feel that way?"

"We don't. I was just happy is all. I sure hope we find that Hummer. It's the last key to this mystery."

"We won't unless we leave the parking lot," she hinted, to which I tore out of the drive, swerving onto US 23. "And you talk about my driving," she giggled. "Where should we go now? I mean how on earth are we ever gonna figure out where the Hummer is?"

"We'll tool around town, and then if we don't turn up anything, we're gonna head over to the scene of the first crime."

"To where Raul fell to his death?"

"Yes, the Hummer has been spotted there before and maybe it might return."

"For what reason?"

"I just have a feeling is all. Work with me, Eleanor."

She nodded. "Okeydokey, boss."

We passed the motorcycle Grandmas and I rolled down my

window. "Hey! Has anyone seen a Hummer roll past?" I yelled over the roar of the Harleys.

"I seen one pull into the Walmart's parking lot," the one with a pink leather jacket said.

I thanked the ladies and we headed that way. It was easy enough to spot the monstrosity of a vehicle parked in the middle of the lot. When I drove past it, nobody was inside, but on the second roll past, I noticed something unusual. It had a bright yellow bumper sticker that read, *Alien Investigation Team.*

"That can't be a coincidence," El said. "You don't think that crazy alien guy Rob is involved in this case, do you?"

"Well, first he said a Hummer was seen at the house where his apartment is and then said—"

"It flew away," El laughed.

"Maybe it's really a spacecraft and Rob is an alien. It would make sense why he can spot an alien a mile away."

"Or that he was hoping to really throw us off the trail. Maybe he thought if he gave us some crazy story, we'd think he was nuts and move on."

"He is nuts, and it sure worked, because no way would I think this has a thing to do with our case."

I backed into a space not too far from the Hummer and shut off the engine and lights. El and I waited until daylight faded away into darkness. "Figures. It's dark now. My eyesight is no damn good at night."

"Mine either, but there's something else we could do."

"Which is?"

"Wait back at the apartment building to see if they show up."

"Yes, but what if we're wrong and this Hummer never shows up there? We'd lose our only chance at finding out who might really be involved."

"But there's the sticker and—"

"It's not enough. I want to see that snake Rob crawl into that Hummer with my own two eyes. I'm convinced that he's at the bottom of this."

El slinked down in her seat. "Well, you won't have to wait much longer because there he is."

Sure enough, Rob Glasier and an unidentified man were carrying bags, and climbed into the Hummer. We followed it to the same house Rob's apartment was at... the scene of the first crime. I found a place to park a block away and El and I called Sheriff Peterson. The call went straight to voicemail and I left a message at the tone. "Looks like we're all alone on this one," I said.

"What's the plan?"

"We're gonna sneak in the front door and check out this lead."

"Maybe we should wait for Peterson," El suggested.

"I left him a message, and at this point we don't know anything for sure. If only Peterson had shared more information with us earlier."

We snuck up to the house and I searched for a spare key. El opened the mailboxes that were simply five metal boxes, and found a spare key in the one labeled with Raul Perez's name. I had to contain my excitement as I used the key to enter the front door. We each slid in through the door and froze for a few minutes as we stood in complete darkness. It wasn't safe to turn on the lights, so I used my cell phone light. We crept up the steps, freezing when one creaked out. When nobody came into the hallway, we followed the sound of voices coming from Rob's apartment.

The voices were easily heard through the door. "I told you not to worry. I tied up our last loose end. The police think Harry killed Raul and Maria and then himself."

"What about those old ladies? What if they keep meddling?"

"Don't worry about them. There's no way anyone would think I'm involved."

"But, Rob, I'm just not so sure."

"Stop being such a sissy. All we have to do is wait a few months and then hire a lawyer. Folks in town will have all but forgotten about Raul, Maria, and Harry."

"How do you plan to convince them you're Maria's son?"

"Oh that's simple. I have documentation from the orphanage Maria dumped me in. I'll be established as the only heir and will inherit the beach house."

My mind swirled. Rob was Maria's son? He was responsible for the deaths of three people. I jerked upright and tripped down a few steps. The door swung open and we were yanked into the room.

"Help!" El screamed at the top of her lungs.

A gun was shoved in El's face. "Shut your trap," Rob said, with glazed over eyes.

I panted loudly. All I could think about was how El and I were in danger and might perish. "You're Maria Sanchez's son, aren't you?"

"You're quite the little eavesdropper, but I guess it doesn't matter now, so yes. She placed me up for adoption when I was a baby and it took me over thirty years to find her, but when I did, I found out she was listed as a beneficiary on a piece of property on Lake Huron."

"She told you that? Why?"

"Raul had just died the day before, and she was distraught. She blabbered on about many things, about her affairs with both Raul and Harry. That she drugged Raul the day he died and then pushed him to his death. She figured with Raul out of the way, her and Harry could live happily ever after in the beach house. His wife would even have to pay alimony. They'd be set for life. Harry had stolen the money from his wife to buy the beach house and she was none the wiser."

"So you lied when you said you saw a tall thin man push Raul to his death?"

"And you sucked it up, like I knew you would. Like I'd believe you two old bats were in the Air Force."

El swallowed hard. "I guess you have us pegged."

My eyes widened at his harsh tone and I refocused on Raul's involvement with the purchase of the beach house. "I figured as much. I knew Raul just didn't have the necessary funds to buy that house."

"I know the money to buy the beach house was given to Maria, so why did she give it to Raul?"

"Because she figured Raul was more viable. Harry was married and had refused to divorce his wife."

"So what changed?"

"Harry changed his mind and she decided her only way out of the mess was if she killed Raul."

"What an evil bitch!" El spat.

I shook my head. "Why kill Maria then? She'd most likely allow you to stay there rent free."

"Harry didn't see it that way. He thought I was a nut job. He didn't understand the importance of my alien investigations, and that piece of property is important to my research. You have no idea how important it is that we find a viable alien specimen."

"A spacecraft crashed north of East Tawas a few months ago," the mystery man said.

"You mean the asteroid?" El asked.

"That's what they want you to think," Rob spat. "I went down to that site and I saw a tall alien run into the woods with my own two eyes."

I tried hard not to roll my eyes. "Who's your accomplice here?"

"I'm Rob's friend, Ashton. We've been investigating aliens for years now."

"So you found out Maria was living here and came to town to meet her, Rob?"

"Yes. I had no idea what a great opportunity it was for me, until later when she spilled her guts. It was then that I formulated a plan to kill her and make Harry look like the killer. I had to really, because you old bats wouldn't stop poking around and asking questions."

"So you drugged her and left her for dead at the beach?"

"It was the perfect plan. Harry had been sharing his prescriptions for Oxycodone with her for weeks. I didn't leave her for dead; she died from the overdose I gave her. Harry freaked out after that, and I convinced him to meet me at the Northland Cabins—"

"Did he suspect you of murdering Maria?"

"Of course not! It's not like he was there."

"So why did he agree to meet you?"

"I told him I'd give him the beach house after it was probated," he laughed. "I still can't believe he thought it would be that easy. That I'd actually do that, give him something that is rightfully mine."

"And you overdosed him as well and wrote a suicide note."

"Yes."

Eleanor gasped. "How did you get him to take the pills, is what I want to know!"

"Simple, I dissolved them in his whiskey. He said it tasted strange at first, but he was so distraught that it wasn't hard to convince him to drink."

I shook my head. "There is just no way the sheriff was buying these deaths as accidental. You should have thought about the toxicology reports. I'm sure it will only be a matter of time before Harry's toxicology report comes out and it will all look too much like a coincidence."

"You're wrong here. It's completely believable that Harry killed both Raul and Maria in a fit of jealous rage."

"Maybe," I said. "That is until you showed up trying to claim the property as your own. Probate is a lengthy process and they'd put up the property for sale."

Rob clenched his hands into fists. "Not always. Sometimes they put the house into the name of the heir."

"Did you consult a lawyer here? Because I think you're wrong. Once the house went into probate the cops would be all over it. Don't think they wouldn't be watching and waiting."

"It wouldn't matter because they would have to prove it, something they just can't do."

"You're a fool. Alien investigation my patootie. You're more nuts than I thought if you think you can get away with this."

I walked for the door with a wide-eyed El looking on. Rob put his gun against the back of my head. "Freeze, lady!"

"Now, no need to act crazy here," El said.

I tugged my right earlobe and El reached into her bag, coming back with a Taser. She shot Rob with it, but he only went to his knees... his eyes wide and bulging... the gun shaking, but still clutched in his hand. I squeezed my eyes shut as the gun he held was cocked back. The door swung open next and we raced for the door as the military woman next door, Trish Gunner, stood at the door with one of her grenades in her hand. She pulled the pin and with wide eyes tossed it under a table.

El and I ran screeching down the hallway, our clumsy feet slipping and sliding down the steps as Trish followed us. "Hurry up girls, before he realizes it's a dummy grenade."

When I whipped open the door, Sheriff Peterson was racing toward the door, with Trooper Sales in his wake. I rattled off what had happened and they whizzed past us, barking off orders to stay outside. I rested against the railing and tried to regain my composure. Bubble lights from ten cop cars lit up the night sky and passerbys gawked in disbelief.

"Thanks, Trish," I finally said. "I thought we were goners."

"I heard a woman scream, and when it wasn't Bessie across the hall, I bided my time until I decided I had better intercede before he offed one of you ladies. That guy is nuts!"

"Yes, can you believe he actually thinks aliens crash landed nearby?"

"He watches too much television," Trish said. "I always knew he was off, but I had no idea he'd resort to killing his own mother and her lover."

"You sure can hear pretty good through that door," El said with a snicker.

"Well, these walls are mighty thin," she agreed.

A half an hour later, Rob and his friend Ashton were hauled out the front door and into Sheriff Peterson's cruiser. Sheriff Peterson nodded at us. "You both okay?"

"I tried to call you," I said.

"I know. Next time wait for the Calvary," he said with a wink before making his way to his cruiser.

Andrew arrived in full protective mode and gave me a hug. Words at this point weren't necessary. All I knew was that El and I had dodged a bullet once again.

Epilogue

We were once again on the deck of Hidden Cove restaurant. It was nearly dusk, and a waitress had just set down drinks for Trooper Sales and Sheriff Peterson who had just joined the party dressed in plain clothes. Also in attendance were Mr. Wilson and Eleanor. Andrew sat next to me, closer than he had since he came back to town, but then again we weren't teenagers. Martha stood near the railing with her flavor of the month, Curtis Hill. I was surprised at her choice this time around, but she really enjoyed going four-wheeling with Curtis. Rosa Lee Hill smiled at me from across the deck and raised her drink at me as she stood next to her son, Curt, and Sally Alton who he had recently started dating.

Just this morning Kimberly Steele had picked up Mr. Tinkles, or Weenie as she called him. Eleanor had resigned herself to the fact that the dog just didn't belong to her. Who knows? Maybe Eleanor needed a pet of some sort. Maybe I'd buy her a goldfish.

S.S. Murphy left town, promising to return when her legal team had their case ready, as she had planned to make waves, since her stolen money was used to buy the beach house. It sure would be sad if the state were able to confiscate the property.

"It sure was surprising about how Clay Barry withdrew for the election like that," I said to Peterson.

He raised a brow. "It sure was. You know anything about that, that you're willing to share?"

I sipped my wine, and then said, "Nope. Some things are better left unsaid. Don't you agree?"

"I sure do. My father, Hal, is moving in to an assisted living facility in town. He likes it much better than the nursing home, but I think it's best he be looked after a little more closely. I'm afraid my wife, Joy, was about ready to divorce me if he stayed with us much longer. I'm glad the judge only gave him probation for using Raul

Trouble in Tawas

Perez's credit card."

"That's fair." I kept my lip closed about how they should have just dropped the charges. "I heard that the older woman, Bessie, who was staying across the hall from Rob was picked up by her son. It's so nice she doesn't have to stay in an apartment like that."

"She's Cat Lady's sister," Peterson informed us, and in a big way I believed that.

"So what of Rob and Ashton?" Eleanor asked. "Are they getting off on some insanity plea?"

"Nope, they both plead guilty to murder charges. I hear they think aliens now inhabit the prison they're at. It's created quite a stir, and they are actively investigating as prisoners."

"I always knew that man was nuts. You don't believe in aliens, do you, Andrew?" I asked.

Before he had a chance to answer, we all watched in wonder as a shooting star lit across the sky and tumbled into Lake Huron.

About the Author

Madison Johns began writing at the age off 44 without any prior education or formal training. Although sleep deprived from working third shift, she knew if she used what she had learned while caring for senior citizens to good use, it would result in something quite unique. In 2012 she unleashed her first Agnes Barton mystery, Armed and Outrageous, onto the publishing scene opting to become an independent author. In has gone on to be her first Amazon bestseller.

In 2013 she published two other books in the Agnes Barton series and they like the first, have went on to become bestsellers in both the cozy mystery and humor categories. Her Agnes Barton series features two senior aged ladies digging up clues with enough laugh aloud antics to cause James Bond to blush. It features zany and quirky characters that are easy to fall in love with.

She has also published a romance novella, Pretty and Pregnant, in 2013. In October of 2013, Tirgearr Publishing published her romance novel, Redneck Romance.

Madison is now able to do what she loves best and work from home as a full time writer. She has two children and black lab to keep her company while she churns out more Agnes Barton stories with a few others brewing in the pot.

Madison is a member of sisters in crime.
Sign up for Madison Johns' newsletter.
https://www.facebook.com/MadisonJohnsAuthor/app_100265896690345
Or check out her on Facebook
https://www.facebook.com/MadisonJohnsAuthor
Website
http://madisonjohns.com

Printed in Great Britain
by Amazon